To Dream of a Highlander

SAMANTHA HOLT

Copyright © 2014 Samantha Holt

All rights reserved.

ISBN: 1499535090
ISBN-13: 978-1499535099

CONTENTS

Acknowledgments

Prologue	5
Chapter One	8
Chapter Two	33
Chapter Three	71
Chapter Four	106
Chapter Five	140
Chapter Six	174
Chapter Seven	205
Chapter Eight	226
Chapter Nine	255
Chapter Ten	276
Epilogue	295

ACKNOWLEDGMENTS

Thank you, Jenny, Summer and Tina. These people know why! Lots of love to Tonya, who has supported me from very close to the beginning. All of you encourage me to push forwards, to overcome bumps in the road and continue the crazy journey of being a writer.

A huge thank you also to my readers. I appreciate every single one of you for joining me in my imaginary world.

PROLOGUE

"Ye must take her place, Catriona."

Catriona propped her hands on her hips and tilted her head to view the large man. A breeze blew through the open windows of the solar and she shuddered. "What is yer meaning, Father?"

Laird Malcolm swiped a hand across his damp upper lip and glanced out of the thin window. "Yer sister's betrothed shall be sending men to fetch her."

"Well, they shall have a surprise when they find out she is dead," she scoffed, immediately regretting it as he snapped his head around, expression menacing.

Her father snatched her arm, squeezed tight. "Dinnae speak back to me, child. Much is riding on yer sister's match to Laird Gillean. I want ye to go with the men to Kilcree. Pretend to be Katelyn."

Catriona stared into those dark, soulless eyes, the usual dart of dread slashing at her stomach. But still she kept her voice strong. "And what would ye have me do? Marry the laird?"

"Nay, 'twill not come to that. I shall have the king's support by then and I can end the contract without fear of retribution. Ye just need to appease him for a wee while until there are enough men on Bute to see off any attack."

"Father, this is folly. He shall know I am not Katelyn. I am naught like her."

He squeezed her arm once more. "That I well know. Ye could have learned a lot from Katelyn. She had no soft notions. Ach, it vexes me that I lost my dutiful daughter only to be left with ye."

Catriona narrowed her eyes but said nothing, well used to her father's complaints of her inadequacy. She was not good enough for him. Too soft, no ambition. Well, she'd rather be considered soft than a vile wretch like her sister. Though they were twins, they had never been close. Catriona tried to feel guilty for such thoughts but she failed. The lass never had a kind word to say to anyone.

"Do ye want to see war brought to Bute?" her father pressed, running a hand through his dark grey hair.

She sagged. "Nay, of course not."

"Then do this for me. Be yer sister for but a few sennights and I shall send for ye once the isle is secure. We can break off the marriage contract and ye can return. My daughters—" he sighed, "*daughter* was not born so beautiful to be married off to such a man. I have better plans for ye now. So what say ye? Shall ye protect this island and do yer duty?"

CHAPTER ONE

Battle cries and the clash of swords on armour resounded through the bailey. A burst of nerves surged through her. Catriona peered out of the window of the round castle and her stomach roiled. For three days, they'd kept the Norsemen at bay with boiling resin and molten lead but their efforts were for nothing. With strong shields, the invaders protected themselves and hacked away at the new ramparts.

"They will break through at any moment," Catriona whispered to herself.

Her father had only begun erecting the keep some fifteen summers past a while after he took the isle from the Norse. But now they were back at the walls, determined to take back the land for themselves.

Swiping clammy hands over her skirts, she inhaled slowly. Bute Keep would fall to the Norse soon enough and there would be little hope for her—a mere woman.

A chunk of stone pinged through the open window as an arrow struck not far from her viewing point. She darted inside and scanned her sister's chambers, nose wrinkled. The smell of death clung to the air, even though it had been four sennights since she had passed. Catriona pressed her lips together. While her sister had never been kind, Catriona would not wish the ravages of dysentery on anyone. It was a strange sight—her twin wasting away, devoured by sickness. She wrapped her arms about herself. Mayhap it was better Katelyn had died. Should the Norse have got their hands on her, she knew not what they would have done.

A shiver tripped down her spine.

She would fare just as badly.

She needed to escape. But how? The keep was surrounded, the fighting fierce. She risked death by stepping outside the upper chambers. Her father had told her to remain inside. Catriona swallowed the knot in her throat. She'd heard enough tales of Norse barbarity. Rapes, pillaging. Was this what they were to expect? Would she die this day?

With a final glance around the room, she made her decision. She would not die here, cowering and quivering, with the acrid scent of death in her nostrils as night fell around them. Hurrying to the door, she twisted the handle, grimacing as the iron squeaked. She peered through the small gap. A whistle of air. The sounds of dying men and crumbling masonry. But no enemy. Skirts in hand, she scurried along the corridor and followed the spiral steps down to the hall.

No one paid any heed to her but Catriona saw everything she needed to. The men-at-arms had retreated into the castle and were busy shoring up the defences of the hall. Laird Malcolm, her father, directed the men to place strong wooden beams across the entrance.

Catriona shook her head. For all the good it would do them. Those doors were not strong enough to hold back a horde of Norsemen—or Vikings as the men referred to them. Slippers crunching across the rushes, she made her way to the kitchen stairs and descended. A few men and women cowered behind the large oak table.

"Lady Catriona," the cook hissed, standing and weighing a cooking knife in his hand. "Come, lass, and hide."

"Nay, I'll no' stay here. The enemy will break through at any moment."

The big ruddy man snorted. "And where shall ye go, wee Catriona? Ye'll no' survive out there." He motioned with his knife out of the small rear door.

"I'll seek shelter with the villagers."

"If ye can even reach them. Ye'll be spotted by a Viking for sure. Dinnae be foolish. A lass like ye is a fine prize for a lusty Viking."

She stiffened at this, aware her looks had brought her much unwanted attention over the years. Since she had come of age many men had tried to sway her into bed. While her sister relished the attention, she did not. She would not give herself up so readily to a Norseman.

"Pray come with me," she implored as crashing sounded above and several women released sounds of distress.

"Nay. 'Tis guaranteed death to go out there. Here, we stand a chance."

Catriona suppressed a frustrated curse. Did they not see it was better to at least try? Mayhap they would be well, she told herself as she spun away.

"Good luck to ye, lass," Cook murmured behind her.

Pressing through the door, she blew out a heavy breath. She refused to cower and await death. The men-at-arms had been talking of what might happen should the Norse break through—some of them cruelly teasing her with tales. A few whom she had declined took particular delight in describing how a Viking planned to take his pleasure with her.

Catriona closed the door and flattened her back against it, willing her imaginings away. Hopefully the servants would remain unharmed but a lass like herself... she'd had troubles enough over her years. She would not stay to discover if the tales were true.

Her father would be furious to find her gone, but she cared little what he thought. He only wanted her to continue their ruse. The household knew of their plan and she had been playing at being Lady Katelyn for any visitors to Bute since her sister's death, while they waited for word from Katelyn's betrothed. Until the Norse landed on their shores, that was.

Breath held, the clatter of swords and footsteps grew close. The stickiness on her palms increased and she smoothed them over her gown. Her chest constricted. Someone approached down the narrow corridor leading out of the kitchen and to the rear of the keep. Her escape was blocked.

She clamped a hand over her mouth to stifle a cry. Shouts sent a shiver through her, the fear clawing up her throat making it almost impossible to breathe. Shadows slithered across the walls, distorted by the few lit torches. How had the Norsemen found the secret passage? Should she go back into the kitchen? Nay, if she did, she would lead them directly to the rest of the household. Her only choice was to confront the invaders.

Trembling, she edged away from the door and followed the curve of the passageway.

It seemed to Catriona that a wild, brawling mass of limbs and armour had plunged into the small space. She no longer had trouble breathing but her body failed her—left her frozen. She stood as still as prey beneath a hawk while the stench of sweat and blood assaulted her.

His foreign appearance, the long hair and unusual clothing startled her and a hand clenched around her arm, snapping her out of her daze. A squeak escaped her, a noise that should have been a scream should her throat have cooperated. Body shaking, she dragged her gaze fearfully up to meet the cold blue of the Norseman's eyes. Was it horror playing with her mind or was he truly the size of a giant?

He thrust her against the wall, causing her head to crack against the stone while he muttered something in his foreign tongue. Catriona noted the blood on his hands had transferred to her gown. The blood of the soldiers of Bute. How bad had the slaughter been?

His blood slickened hand travelled up to her face to curl around her cheek. A cry threatened to spill from her mouth but she held it at bay. She failed to supress her shudder as his rancid breath washed over her. Reluctantly, she dragged her gaze to his. Mayhap if she begged…? But, nay, the frigidness still lingered in his eyes. She only hoped he ravished her and left her be. She steeled her resolve. The sea of nausea in her stomach ebbed.

"Do what ye will," she whispered, closing her eyes.

The clang of his sword on stone rang in her ears, the rattle echoing against the walls—and through her mind. The Norseman rubbed his thumb over her cheek. Catriona felt the smear of blood from his hand and whimpered. He thrust his other hand under her hair and held it tight, forcing her head back and sending shooting pains through her scalp.

"*Du er vakker*," he growled and she drew open her lids.

Her breaths grew ragged as her mind whirled. Was there any way to get away from the huge man? She had no weapons, no great fighting skill. If she could just catch him at a vulnerable moment, could she escape? She wriggled against the hold on her hair and winced as he yanked it harder. Nay, there was no escaping him now. She had to wait. The attention she garnered had always made her uncomfortable but she knew well how to fend off advances with teasing and bold words. If she played the temptress, mayhap there would be opportunity for escape.

This thought—this idea that she could be in control—sent up a wall around her heart, but would it give way as softly as the stone of Bute Keep? Her fear drained away. Was this what warriors felt before war? Warmth entered her limbs, her bones may have been made of steel. She stood strong and met his gaze.

A grin twitched on his lips. "You would like a Viking between your thighs, *nei*?"

Catriona only managed to nod slowly, not trusting her voice to work. She clenched her hands into fists, barely concealing a tremor, as he pressed his lips to her neck. Dampness trailed over her skin, unwelcome hands clutched her gown, the odour of sweat and pungent breath reeled about her.

In and out.

She focused on breathing. *In and out.* Coarse fingers came to the neckline of her gown and tugged. When the Norseman kissed the curve of her breast, her breaths quickened. The brush of prickly beard and the sight of his fair head upon her chest began to chip away at the wall. Slowly her defences were crumbling—like that of the castle. The realisation that she could not survive this raider invading her body made her palms damp, her blood soar through her veins. The pounding of alarm through her urged her to flee or fight.

She managed to rein in her terror long enough for him to drop to his knees and hoist her skirts. Those blood-tinged fingers pinched the flesh of her thighs as they slithered their way to her juncture. Unable to bear it any longer—and silently praying this moment would be her salvation—she brought her knee up into his face with all the strength her panic-ridden limbs could muster.

A sharp shout came from the man—a word that sounded like a curse, and he dropped back and clutched his nose. Catriona flitted her gaze desperately around while blood seeped from between his fingers and his eyes hardened. She could not flee until the man was rendered senseless. He still stood between herself and escape. But she had nothing with which to defend herself.

She tried to press past him but strong hands wrapped around her waist and hauled her back against the wall. A fist to her face sent the world spinning and fiery pain flared through her cheek.

His leather armour squeaked while he positioned himself, forcing her thighs apart with a painful grip. Somehow Catriona muffled her scream while she fought and thrashed against the giant. Tears dripped freely down the sides of her face. Rape—maybe death—was all that awaited her now.

One hand pinned her wrists above her head, while the other concentrated on yanking up her heavy skirts. Still she whipped about. Whatever he took, he would not take easily. Defeat beat heavily in her breast but she refused to give up yet.

Her attacker pressed back briefly to free himself and something warm splattered across her chest. The grip on her wrists loosened and Catriona blinked as the Viking's wrathful expression turned to one of confusion. He made a gargling sound as more liquid spilled onto her and the tip of a sword burst from his chest. Holding back the scream that tore from her throat proved impossible this time as the point hovered close to her own chest. The Viking fell away and clutched the wound as the blade withdrew. Scrabbling away, she looked on in horror as his head dropped and he collapsed to the floor. Any relief she may have felt was replaced with shaking terror when a larger Viking took his place. He sheathed his sword and eyed her.

"Who are ye?" he demanded.

His brogue confused her. A native of one of the western isles perhaps?

"I-I am Lady Katelyn." The words tumbled out before she considered it. Why keep up the lie for this Viking? Yet, she could not let the truth out, not even to her enemy. Not when Gillean, Katelyn's betrothed, might add to Bute's troubles.

Catriona tried not to sob. All her fighting had been for nothing. She would never hold off *this* man. His blue gaze flicked over her and he lunged forward and snatched her into his hold.

"Come with me," he ordered before throwing her over his shoulder.

The pain in her cheek muddled her thoughts but she still fought his grip. Catriona clawed at his back, fingernails cracking against his leather armour. His shoulder winded her as he hefted her into a firmer hold, strong arm clamped tightly around her. Desperation seared through her while her kicks weakened. The blow to her face must have done more damage than she thought. Vision blurred, her stomach lurched and blood pounded into her face. She was weakening. Who knew what would happen now? The Viking was already carrying her out of the rear of the castle. Everything passed in a haze. Shouts and the scrape of swords were distant now and she realised she was losing her senses. Where was he taking her?

Time slipped by in ebbs. It seemed that suddenly they

were far from the keep, the lush green of the island grass shooting past her. Her kidnapper's gait was fast and sure but at times it felt as if she were suspended in time, her thoughts growing more confused, limbs becoming weak. If she could only fight the brute of a man. Grey rocks appeared to come too close to her head as he descended the slowly rolling hills. Catriona suspected they were headed toward the coast.

To return to Norway?

Once, a long time ago, the Norsemen kidnapped Scots women and took them to their homeland, never to be seen again. Mayhap she was to be a prize of war.

Shingle crunched under his boots. They were by the sea. The man stopped and her heart tripped. Suddenly the arm around her loosened and she plummeted down. Rough wood met her rear and she scrabbled to right herself. Sitting in the damp bottom of a small boat, Catriona glanced fearfully around at the men surrounding her, all sat on benches and ready to row. Her throat grew dry and tight, and she considered screaming. For what though? No aid would come.

He climbed into the boat and Catriona blinked up at him. The huge fair warrior barely glanced at her as he stepped over the benches and shouted to the men in his unusually fluent Gaelic.

"We must away—with haste. Dusk will be upon us soon."

When he faced her, Catriona was unable to prevent

herself from scurrying back, nearly knocking into one of the other men's bare leg. But instead of grabbing her or threatening her, he simply smiled. His strong features lit with the grin.

Gaze skipping from man to man as the grey light of dusk settled over them, she rose and peered over the edge of the boat. They were not yet away from the beach. Another man had jumped out to push the boat from the shoal. There was still a chance for escape.

Catriona stood abruptly, making the vessel rock and prepared to jump overboard.

***

Finn glanced behind him, noting the hazy flicker of light on the hills. Either a fire had been lit in an attempt to burn out the defenders or the Norse had taken the keep and were in full command now, lighting the torches and readying to claim the island as theirs.

They were not yet out of danger. He couldn't even be sure they would be safe on the mainland. The Norse boats were surely quicker than their small vessel and more heavily manned. Once they realised the lady of the keep was gone, they might look for her.

He scrubbed a hand over his face. How exactly had he become embroiled in all this?

Oh, aye, his wee sister of course. A lady he could never deny. Under pressure from her brother by marriage to gather men and rescue his betrothed, she had asked for his aid. Ach, but Laird Gillean would never risk his own life for a lass, Finn thought bitterly. Originally the laird had planned to fetch Lady Katelyn off the isle himself but when it became apparent the Norse invasion was imminent, he was conveniently called away on business, leaving Lorna with few men to carry out such a duty. But how could a brother ignore the imploring missive of a sister?

He swivelled to glance over their precious bundle. The lass cowered and looked at him as if he were some strange creature. It was to be expected. No doubt her mind was somewhat addled after her experience. She clearly had no knowledge of warfare and no woman should have to go through near ravishment. Finn curled his fist at the memory of seeing that rancid excuse for a warrior mounting her. Ach, but at least he had the satisfaction of having drawn the man's blood. Never again would he touch any of the fine Scottish lassies.

About to turn and take his seat, a movement caught his eye. He lunged forward as Katelyn stood and took a step over the side of the boat. They were still practically on the shore so she landed in the soft sand with ease, just out of Finn's reach, water lapping at her thighs.

Calling her name, he leaned over the edge and cursed as the vessel rocked. The foolish lass was going to get them wet and not all the men were able to swim. Regardless of the depth, if there was a strong tide they'd be pulled out to sea. She darted a fearful glance at him and gripped her skirts.

He saw the desire to run but why?

He readied himself to leap over but a sharp wave caught the boat, tossing him into the hull. Grumbling, he came to his feet once more only to see Lady Katelyn had vanished. He looked to the other men in the boat but they were still readying their oars and getting set for their journey.

"Curse ye, ye fools. The lady has gone overboard!"

The men swivelled, shouts of dismay falling from their lips and Finn shook his head. Shrugging out of his furs, he leaped nimbly over the side. The water bit at his feet through his leather boots and sloshed wildly around his legs. The push and pull of the waves tugged at him as they lapped at the island. With her heavy skirts, it was no wonder she had gone under.

He swung his gaze around, grateful the night had not yet swallowed them. A flash of green a few feet in front of him caught his eye. Hair swirling about her, gown waving like seaweed in the wash, she floated on the surface—knocked senseless.

"Damnation!"

With several strong strides, he caught up with her. The tide drew her away but it was not strong enough to defeat him. The sea now up to his hips, he dragged Katelyn into his arms. By God, her gown weighed her down. Even for a man of his strength, he felt as though he were carrying a heavy sack of grain rather than a sylph of a woman.

Wading to the boat, he hefted her out of the water and passed her to Logan. The man shook his head. "Sorry, Finn. We were concentrating on not getting tossed about in the wash. 'Tisnae easy holding such a small vessel steady."

"Aye, have no fear. 'Twas my fault. The lass has clearly had a shock and I should have been watching her more closely."

Logan laid her in the bow while Finn clambered in. He knelt by the lass and glanced up at Logan.

"She must have taken a hit to the head."

"Aye, likely against the boat. Must have hit hard to render her senseless."

Finn nodded. "Let us get on our way. We can do no good for her here."

"Aye," Logan agreed and backed away to help row the boat from the shoreline.

Leaning over her, Finn studied the gash on her forehead with a grimace. Poor lass. She'd have a mighty fine headache when she awoke. The steady rise and fall of her breasts against the soaked green wool assured him no permanent damage had been done.

"Ye'll have to get her out of those wet garments," Logan called out behind him.

Finn clenched his teeth. "Aye, thank ye, Logan. I'm aware o' that."

He ran his gaze over her. Damn his luck. He'd undressed many a fine woman but none had ever been out cold and an unwilling partner. No doubt the lady would be deeply ashamed he'd done as much. But he could hardly leave her to die from exposure. If anything, his sister would have his head.

Fingers tentatively prying at the front of her bodice, he forced his gaze onto the wood just behind her head. But the wet fabric proved too hard to tug apart so he pressed his hands to her back and lifted her lifeless form. Icy skin and sumptuous curves flattened briefly to his chest as he fumbled with the ties at the back of her gown. By God, when had he ever blundered like a whelp when undressing a woman? But he had to admit, though he'd had little time to admire her and the swelling on her face did not reveal her features properly, the flash of creamy skin was tempting enough. In other circumstances—and had she been anyone other than a lady in distress—he'd have enjoyed such a sight.

He had her face pressed into his neck as he pulled her gown from her. Soft skin under his fingertips forced his breath to stilt. Only the grunts of men rowing reminded him he was meant to be helping the lass and not enjoying the moment.

Katelyn's chemise and gown came away in one go and he peered behind him, narrowing his eyes at the men. "Keep yer eyes away," he warned, "or I'll be having yer heads."

A rumble of chuckles rippled from them but they kept their gazes ahead while he pried the garments from her shoulders. He laid her down, fumbling for his fur to cover her. Unfortunately he failed to keep his gaze from straying briefly to her curves, so pale and lush in the dimming light. Finn thrust the furs over her as his body tightened. Working beneath the pelt, he hauled her gown down her stomach and hips. It should have made it easier—he didn't have to resist temptation to stare at her—but it made him all the more aware of her shapely hips and delicate thighs. Gaze lifted to the heavens, he gritted his teeth, tugged the gown the rest of the way off and slung it aside.

He eyed her for a moment, breath held in his chest as he studied the dark hair as black as night splayed across the wood. Milky skin contrasted with the brown of the pelt. A more tempting sight he had never seen. And there was something familiar about her. Something that tugged at his gut. He'd never met Lady Katelyn and yet her fragrance and slightly husky voice, and mayhap her body played in his mind, as though she were an old lover.

Rolling his eyes at himself, Finn tucked the fur around her. It had simply been too long since he'd had a satisfying tumble. From the time when his dream lass had begun to plague him, no other woman had been able to match her. Mayhap that was what struck him as familiar about this lass. Though the woman in his dreams always appeared hazy, he knew she had hair like a raven.

Ach, he needed to turn his thoughts away from tumbling lassies and concentrate on the task at hand—ensuring they made it safely to his sister's keep. He sank heavily onto a seat and dragged off his boots, grunting with dissatisfaction as he tipped the water out of them. He drew off his trews, grateful to be rid of the clinging wet fabric and motioned for Logan to hand him his plaid and the rest of his garments. He changed while they started away from the coast. His heart still beat rapidly, aware the enemy might be upon them soon. Or was it from the memory of her skin beneath his fingers? They still tingled.

A shuffle and a tiny moan drew his attention. She clutched the pelt around her and fought to sit. "Pray, dinnae harm me. I will do whatever ye wish."

Finn stood sharply, prepared for her to fall into a swoon once more. He propped his hands on his hips and furrowed his brow. Ach, but the lass was more confused than he'd realised.

He'd been abrupt with her to be sure, but surely she understood he was here to help. Finn peered at his precious cargo and noted the woman's shuddering. Curses, where were his manners? The actions of the Viking—and himself—had no doubt terrified the woman. Fiery bloodlust that had pushed him to run her attacker through now simmered to a gentle burn and remorse struck him.

"I've no intention of harming ye." Tension made the statement come out sharper than he'd planned but he'd not expected to have to disguise himself and rescue her mid-siege. When he'd agreed to rescue the lady from the Isle of Bute, he'd intended to reach her before the Norse invaders arrived.

Unfortunately inclement weather and strong winds had brought the attackers across the sea sooner than they'd anticipated. Still, once they made it to his sister's castle all would be well. As long as they survived the journey to the mainland and to Kilcree, he could consider this a successful rescue.

The spatter of the sea tickled his face and he glanced at the steadily disappearing shoreline. The journey to the mainland was a short one but these seas were unpredictable and they were losing light. If they were unlucky, they could be dashed upon the rocks as they came to shore or tossed from their boat.

Gingerly, he stepped forward. She yelped and tucked her

body up into as tiny a shape as possible. Finn shook his head to himself. The poor lass. He crouched beside her. The swelling on her face disguised her features but her long dark hair spilled around her shoulders, like raven's wings. A pang of something struck him sharp in the gut. Mayhap it was anger at her treatment, mayhap it was something else. He refused to dwell on it.

Shuffling closer, Finn inched his fingers under hers and brought her hand to his lips. He smirked. Too late to be playing the gentleman but he would try. Her tiny gasp as he brushed his lips over her cold, slender fingers did something to his chest. It felt as if someone danced a merry jig over his heart. He wanted to hear the sound again. But when he moved nearer still, her eyes widened and she released a long breath as her body fell limp. He barely caught her as she swooned sideways. With a muttered curse, he laid her back down and tucked her in once more.

Finn stared at the woman, retreated and rubbed the back of his neck with his hand. He hadn't expected that reaction. Christ, her ordeal had taken its toll more than he realised. He glanced at Logan, who rowed just behind him, and Logan shrugged. This was unchartered territory for them.

Finn eased himself to his feet and brushed his hands down his plaid. Just went to show how much he knew about lasses.

"How goes it?" Logan asked.

Finn turned to the dark-haired man—and his sister's most trusted aide. "She is fatigued mostly I think. We should allow her to rest now. We still have many miles to cross."

"This was a fool's errand, Finn. Yer lucky ye werenae spotted and killed."

"Ach, I've been told time and again I could pass for a Norseman. 'Twas time to put such looks to use."

"Aye, but going in on yer own... Yer sister would have had my head had ye come to harm." Logan pulled a strong stroke, as if expelling his anger over such a thought.

"Alas none of ye have the looks of anyone but a highlander. And all is well." He slapped a hand to Logan's shoulder.

"'Twas a near thing, Finn, and ye know it."

"Dinnae dwell on what could have happened, Logan. We have done well here this night." Finn let slip a smile. Since the death of Lorna's husband, Logan had practically taken on the role of laird, not that his sister acknowledged it. Yet he still worried for everyone under his care.

Particularly Lorna.

As did they all. His headstrong sister had determinedly continued to run the keep without a man at her side. Thankfully Lorna had the wit of any man and more backbone than most, and though her husband's brother was not a man of much character, he would protect the keep in which she resided.

Finn eyed their progress with satisfaction. The seas remained calm and no unusual weather looked to be headed in their direction. Now their only worry was the lack of light. The moon shone weakly down on them but would not provide enough light for a safe landing if they made it to the wrong part of the shore.

Finn glanced at Katelyn and noted she shook in her slumber. From cold or fear? He hesitated before coming down beside her. Something about this woman made him uncertain of himself, something he had not felt for a long time. But he refused to see a lass suffer. Dropping fully to his knees, he shuffled closer and pressed a tentative finger to her forehead. She did not awaken and her skin froze his fingertips. He stifled the uncomfortable sensation deep in his chest and flexed a hand.

Gaze averted, he moved close to Katelyn and flattened his palm against the rise of one breast. Though her skin still chilled his hand, a rising heat rushed through him. Underneath the silky skin lay the steady beat of her heart and he allowed his shoulders to relax. She needed rest, nothing more. After such an experience he should not be surprised but she'd shown such courage and determination in trying to escape him and her attacker, he had not thought she'd fall back into a swoon.

Lining himself up with her, he scooted close until her fur wrapped legs were aligned with the crook of his thighs. When he peered up, he saw Logan raise an eyebrow but the man said nothing. Finn draped an arm over the pelt and settled against the uncomfortable wood of the boat.

A mumble dropped from her lips and he lifted his head to see her eyelids flutter. She made no attempt to wriggle from his hold so he dropped his head and held her tight. Katelyn must have been very cold not to fight him on this. She'd already shown such determination. He couldn't fight the grin of admiration spreading across his face. What a lass.

"Forgive me, my lady, ye need body warmth."

She responded with a small sigh, one that had his gut twisting and his body responding to her once more. Ach, but he was in a precarious position. Let her freeze to death or risk frightening her further with his inappropriate behaviour.

"All will be well, lass," he soothed. Her body relaxed further into him and his grin expanded. "We'll have ye to safety soon, never fear. Finn mac Chaluim willnae let any harm come to ye, I swear it."

The sound of gentle breaths somehow broke through the slosh of waves and creak of wood. He nodded with satisfaction. Aye, he must have assured her now. With luck, she'd be singing his praises to Lorna and the lassies always loved a hero.

CHAPTER TWO

A strange squeak echoed through Catriona's head. An ache pounded in her skull and each squeak made it worse. Why in God's name was her bed making such a sound? She wriggled but found herself pinned, a substantial weight holding her down by her stomach. She grumbled and twisted again but to no avail. Then she became aware of a heavy puff across her neck. She stiffened.

Male breaths.

She wrenched open her eyes and the throb in her head increased. Dark damp wood surrounded her. A brown fur covered her body and... and a large arm encircled her waist. Breaths growing rapid, she fought the rising surge of panic and forced herself to consider her surroundings properly. The day had turned to night at some point and only slivers of moonlight seeped into the small boat. She could not view the men rowing without drawing attention to herself but she heard the odd low mutter between them and the splash of their oars.

Whoever had her restrained was a large man. Was it the Viking who had taken her? His thighs pressed up against the back of hers and his head rested near her neck—intimately. Her chin wobbled as the haze in her mind cleared. Her clothing was gone. Only the pelt separated her naked body from the warrior. Had he undressed her? Or...or done something else to her? A sound of anguish scrabbled up her throat and she fastened a hand over her mouth.

Catriona considered her body. Aside from the ache in her head and cheek from where the other man had hit her, she did not hurt anywhere else. It was unlikely he had ravished her. Something to be grateful for at least. But now what? She was naked, most likely in the middle of the ocean and trapped in the hold of a vicious warrior. She'd seen the way he'd run that Norse invader through. If he would do that to his own people, what would he do to her?

It was odd for even though she'd studied him momentarily, his eyes had reflected warmth, so very unlike that of the man who'd tried to rape her. No doubt that man would have killed her once he'd had his way. This man, however, had done nothing yet.

Yet.

Just because he had kind blue eyes and an oddly

comforting way of holding her, did not mean he wasn't as vicious as the rest of the Norsemen. Enough tales of their barbarity circulated the castle prior to their invasion. He probably didn't want to ruin her so he could sell her off.

Catriona chewed her lip and concentrated on the waves splashing the hull. Visions of the man against her, his clammy hands pawing her thighs kept threatening to invade her mind. The last thing she needed was her thoughts to be further muddled. And the thought that confused her most? Why did this man's hands upon her—albeit with the furs as a barrier—not send revulsion through her?

A shout brought her kidnapper to his feet and Catriona bunched the furs in one hand, tightening them around her. The boat rocked wildly as the waves swelled beneath them and surf spattered over the boat. Here the scent of salt and seaweed hung strong in the air. They were near the coast, but surely not Norway? She would have known had she been sleeping for that long.

Scooting into a sitting position, she arranged the pelt around her bare legs and peered over the edge of the vessel. Sure enough a beach loomed. Moonlight picked out the hills above them, dusting their tips with silver streams. Catriona scowled and gripped the wood with her free hand. It was the mainland. She knew this place. They must have taken the shortest crossing from Bute to Scotland. But why kidnap her only to bring her to the mainland?

Soon the waves had turned into a seething mass, breaking on the shoreline with a crash. She saw the foamy tips and braced herself as they came closer to the beach. Though the sea was not as rough as some days, bringing a small boat into land was difficult for it was easily tossed about.

She turned and gazed up at the fair man as he directed the men confidently. He stood, legs apart, assured and steady. It seemed as though he was the master of the seas, his confidence unshakable. Surely men bowed to his will. Mayhap he thought the ocean would too?

His deep voice, smooth yet exciting, just reached her ears and she pondered his Gaelic tongue. She had spoken with Norse-Gaels before and many had their own distinct way of speaking but she had never heard any so... so Scottish sounding as he. Catriona blinked as she took a proper study of him. Gone was his fur. Now it likely hung over her shoulders, brushing her bare skin. But what disconcerted her most was his manner of dress. He looked as Scottish as any highlander. Only his shoulder length fair hair made him stand out. And when she looked to the other men, she realised they too wore plaids. Mayhap they always had. Mayhap she had been too horror stricken and disorientated to notice. But for what purpose?

Was she to be part of some great deception? The attack

on Bute was the first after months of discontent on the Norse peoples' part. Bute once belonged to the Norse but the King of Scots wanted the Western Isles back and the King of Norway would have none of it. That did not surprise Catriona. For as long as she had understood men, she had known greediness. But the invasion took them by surprise. None expected the keep to fall.

Sand ground under the hull, making Catriona wince. They had made it through the surf and now the waves fell weakly about the boat. She released a breath, relieved to be on land once more. She did not intend to get soaked again. Once her feet touched the sand, she would consider her next move. Without her garments, she could hardly escape. However, being on the mainland made her chest expand with hope. If she could find a moment to run there would surely be shelter somewhere.

She hoped.

The man jumped deftly over the side and another three men followed. Together they worked to pull the boat fully ashore. Catriona tried to keep her gaze from tracking the tug of his shirt against his muscles but failed repeatedly. He should not, but for some reason the Norseman fascinated her. His features were partially hidden in the gloom of the night but his profile begged her to trace her gaze over it, to follow the sharp lines and dips.

She hunched down when he released his grip on the bow and took a step forward. Gone was her fascination. Now she recalled he had taken her against her will, and there was nothing to prevent him from doing what he wished with her. He offered a hand and she glanced around as her heart threatened to beat out of her chest. She *had* to get out of the boat. *Had* to cooperate for the moment. If she played the meek captive, mayhap they would let their guards down and she could escape. She frowned and slipped her hand into his. Once she got her gown back that was. Catriona squeezed the furs tight at her neck, aware of the breeze swirling about her nude legs.

Feet sinking into the damp sand, she almost groaned aloud. Her slippers were gone, lost in the fight to keep the other attacker from between her thighs. How would she escape without anything on her feet? She eyed the Viking's boots briefly and when she lifted her head she caught him studying her bare legs and feet.

"Ach, ye'll no' get far like that."

In one swift movement, he swept a hand under her legs, the other around her back and scooped her into his arms. Catriona gasped and frantically readjusted the pelt to preserve her modesty.

"Ye dinnae need to...."

"Aye, yer my burden now, lass. Have no fear. I'll no' let

ye come to harm."

Allowing her brow to crease, she gaped at the man. Have no fear? His burden? Did he mean to marry her mayhap? Use her for a political alliance? If he was an important man, a marriage to one of the laird of Bute's daughters would certainly be beneficial.

But, did she believe he did not intend to harm her? Something in his manner was strangely reassuring. The man was a warrior, through and through. Large in stature, strong and sure, but something softer simmered beneath. The way he looked created a tiny fluttering sensation in her chest. She shook her head to swipe away foolish thoughts. She would do well to remember he'd just killed a man and taken her from her home. Whatever he wanted with her did not matter. She had to get away. If he truly meant her no harm, she would be safe until she decided on a way to escape. For the moment, she would be wise to keep her thoughts—and real name and identity—to herself.

"We will make for the hills," he told her, "and set up camp away from the beach. Ye'll get yer gown when it's dry."

She nodded slowly, unable to form any words. His firm hold warmed her cold skin and the thud of his heart against her cheek soothed her. This disconcerted her most of all. In his arms, her shields were down. The flex of his muscles around her body as he took sure steps across the gravelly sand sent heat coiling through her. What a fool she was. She'd heard of lasses being taken and falling in love with their kidnapper. Was this what was happening to her?

The ache in her head forced away any further worries. Little could be done now. She certainly would not be the kind to fall for her enemy and she could ill afford to.

He called to the men behind him, directing them to leave the boat for the owner. The rest of his orders were fuzzy to her ears. Fatigue took its toll, leaching into her limbs and mind. She yawned and was rewarded with a rumbling chuckle. He must have seen it.

"Rest now, wee lass."

Her stomach flipped at his words. What sort of a Viking kidnapper spoke with such tenderness? She failed to supress another yawn. Well, hopefully she would not find out. Once she had rested, she'd get back her gown and make an escape. She would likely never meet the man again.

***

Tèile had watched the boat come into shore. She winced as it tossed about. The seas were calm enough but the wash never made it easy for small boats to land on the beach. There was little to be done about it. If her last experience at matchmaking taught her anything, it was to be more careful with her magic. It would not do to create yet another mess. She huffed to herself and fluttered over them, having to adjust her wings to deal with the slight breeze. Dropping down, she settled on the bow of the boat, using both wings to keep her balance as it rolled with the waves.

She peered at the woman and pondered her. Finn was handsome but his heart was set on staying unmarried. It would prove a task to unite two souls at the right time. Unfortunately she knew little of the woman yet. All the *sidhe* council told her was that she was a lady who would need help. Whatever that meant.

She flexed her wings and sighed. Dealing with mortals was most tiring but the *sidhe* council had commanded it so she had little choice. And she had so hoped she'd be returning home after bringing Alana and Morgann together.

But it appeared she'd used one trick too many. Her weather spells had caused some disturbance and pushed forward the Norse invaders' campaign. Had all gone according to plan, Finn would have met Catriona at a later date and under no guise.

Curses. She could swear the council liked making her life difficult. You'd think they'd be happy she'd achieved her original goal of uniting Morgann and Alana and the two clans. The bloodshed had ceased and the laird and lady were undoubtedly happier than ever.

As the vessel ground to a halt in the sand and a

highlander jumped out to secure it, Tèile dodged out of the way and set her hands determinedly on her hips. She would prove to the council she could do a good job. Then hopefully she would finally be allowed to return home and enjoy the luxuries of the fae world once more.

Her tongue felt dry just thinking of the fae wine she was missing. But she had a job to do. She needed to focus. Soon everyone would be speaking of the Green Faery's great deeds. A grin teased her lips and she thought of the dreams with which she'd already taunted Finn. He might not have realised it yet, but he had met Catriona before. Hopefully the seeds of desire were already planted.

Not quite yet though. She needed to hold them at bay for a little while longer. When the time was right, they would come together in such a clash of love all would be right in the world once more and Tèile could return home.

She let her wings drop. Experience had taught her that mortal hearts were not so easily governed. Tèile prayed she'd learned enough from her last try at matchmaking.

***

As they made their way up away from the beach, Finn glanced at the lass in his arms. He had to keep repositioning the furs as a glimpse of leg or the curve of a breast would peek out. It made concentrating on where he was going more difficult than it should have. Though milky light dotted the hills, the ground was uneven. Thankfully they saw no more of the inclement weather, the green hills remained dry and the clouds had broken apart. A woman in his arms and muddy ground surely spelled trouble so he uttered thanks for the dry grass.

She slept soundly. Over the rush of the sea that whispered through the air, he heard her steady breaths. Katelyn seemed to trust him now which made his chest swell with pride. And then a stab of reality hit him. He did not want or need her trust. Their journey was short enough and then he'd hand her over to his sister—and Katelyn's betrothed—and be on his way. A woman had trusted him once and...

Finn shook his head and glanced at the following men. They walked swiftly, all too aware the Norsemen had probably discovered the lady of the keep was now missing. She would have made a fine prize and a useful bargaining tool with the king. If they wanted her badly enough, the seas were easily crossed. Finn intended to make camp far away from the coastline where their fire could not be seen.

They continued on for several miles until the salty air gave way to the lush scent of heather and grass. With the beach far behind, Finn paused and waited for Logan to catch up. The dark-haired man came to his side and hefted his leather satchel off one shoulder for a moment.

"Are we to make camp?"

Finn nodded. "Aye, we are far enough away I should think. We'll find no shelter here," he glanced around the bare hills, "but we can see many a mile. No thief or bandit will be able to sneak up on us."

"Indeed. The moonlight is strong too. 'Twould be easy to spot a stranger."

"We must count our blessings the skies have cleared. The lass has taken a soaking enough."

"Well the weather is mild enough. She'll no' catch a chill now. Though Lorna willnae be happy ye handled her so."

"What would ye have me do? Ye were the one who suggested removing her garments, or had ye forgotten?" Finn drew back his shoulders and forced aside memories of soft skin beneath his fingertips.

"Aye, but Lorna would tell ye that ye shouldnae have let her get wet in the first place."

"Ach, ye are worse than her, Logan. Too much time at my sister's side, that is yer problem. Ye sound like a nagging lassie."

Logan bristled. "Someone had to stay by her side."

Finn frowned, perturbed by his defensive tone. Lorna was capable of looking after herself, a trait Finn took great pride in. As a brother—and the only male in their direct line—he had a duty to the women in his family. But he took little enjoyment in having a woman dependent on him, even a beloved sister. Women were too fragile and vulnerable. Too easily harmed. It pleased him that Lorna did not depend on him for her safety. That way, he could never fail her like he had Alice.

"Gather some wood and light a fire," he ordered, unwilling to dwell on the subject any longer. Logan huffed and went off in search of firewood as the other men dropped their bags wearily and began making camp.

The crossing had drained them all—rowing against the tide took some strength—so he decided to take first watch. Mayhap it was because he'd been carrying Katelyn or perhaps the thrill of battle still flowed in his blood, because his body remained tense, his senses alert. Ach, how had he ended up doing the one thing he hated—looking after a vulnerable woman? He would far rather be at the MacRae keep in Glencolum with his kin.

He studied the lady and kneeled. Gingerly placing her down, he held his breath as he waited for her to stir. But her breaths came slowly and her eyes remained shut. The exertions of the day had certainly taken their toll. She had appeared fully alert when she'd awoken so he did not think her head injury had caused any permanent damage but it would be an idea to wake her soon to be sure.

Sitting, he rested an arm upon one knee and watched Logan put a flint to the fire. The fire grew quickly, bathing their small camp in a warm glow. Aye, he missed home. Missed his small cottage and simple life. He had been gone just over a sennight but he hungered for his own bed and the company of the good men around his cousin's table. Of course, once Morgann married, life at Glencolum had changed. His duties lessened now Morgann had Alana at his side. In truth, as happy as he was for Morgann, it gave him too much time.

Time to ponder the emptiness of his small cottage. Time to watch their love. Time to wonder... Ach, what was he thinking? He turned his gaze to Katelyn in a search for distraction. While the fire hissed and popped, she slept on. For some reason, he longed to know how she looked without bruises marring her face. Did her features match her body? Delicate in places, yet lush in others. Her lips were full. With a golden glow painting them, they were a tempting sight to be sure. What colour were they in the full light of day? The dim shadows of the keep and the growing dusk had disguised her, piquing his curiosity. But her secrets were not intended for him. Once he took her to Kilcree there would be no reason for him to stay. Another man lay in her future and he would be the one to discover her secrets, to relish in the beauty Finn suspected sat beneath the swollen cheek and puffy eyes.

"I will take first watch," he told Logan as he handed out chunks of bread.

Finn picked at the coarse bread, hard from their travels.

His appetite evaded him but he ate regardless. Katelyn's appearance was testament to the Norse warriors' brutality. He needed his strength. He flexed his fingers and fought the urge to trace the marks on her face. How he longed to run them all through. Even killing her aggressor had done little to assuage his desire for revenge. What kind of men attacked an innocent woman? Unfortunately Finn had seen enough warfare to know it was not uncommon. The years leading up to Alana and Morgann's marriage had been riddled with
strife. Bloodshed did strange things to men.

A small sound emanated from Katelyn and he swallowed when he noticed her shuddering movements. Ach, even with the warmth of the fire and the thick furs, they were not enough to protect her from the elements. A noble woman like her had likely never spent a night outside whereas he'd spent too many. Warriors such as himself barely felt the cold and slept with ease. He also awoke with ease too. Not many would have picked up on the sounds Katelyn made, but his ears were attuned to her every noise. Being so aware of her made his stomach churn.

Duty. It was only duty. Something he'd done his best to avoid. Nevertheless, letting Lorna down was not an option. With a sinking heart, he finished the rest of his bread and slid down next to Katelyn. Carefully, and trying not to disturb the pelt, he slipped an arm underneath her head. His movements slow, he tugged her into him and wrapped his other arm around her. Finn did not worry that he might fall asleep in this position. Indeed his mind blazed with awareness. What caused that, he did not wish to think on.

Katelyn mumbled, her eyelids fluttered and she burrowed her head further into his chest. The woman must have been particularly chilled. He'd never met a noble woman so fearless. Even Alana with her feisty temperament, or Lorna with her bold tongue, would not have tolerated being held by a strange man while wearing no more than a fur. Was it too soon to admire her for her practical nature? The lass had barely said two words yet after her initial fear she accepted his help with great dignity. Many of the lasses he knew might have chosen to freeze to death instead.

Still he felt the need to atone for his conduct. "Forgive me, my lady. Ye were shaking. Ye need body warmth."

"I—thank ye, sir."

And now she thanked him for his behaviour. Lord, she was unlike any lass he'd ever met. Ach, in his experience lasses either played the coy innocent or the uptight noblewoman. He'd eventually broken through all of those acts, he thought to himself with a grin. But Katelyn was different. Mayhap under other circumstances he would have been met with pretence, but he suspected not. Few people fooled him.

"Yer gown shall be dry before long and then ye will have

no more need of me."

She nodded, viewing him from under her lashes. Something unreadable sat behind those eyes. Likely a quick mind worked behind them.

"Are we far inland?"

"Some ten miles."

"Do ye no' fear Scots attacking ye?"

"We hold a strong position and have many powerful sword arms on our side. Ye need not fear, my lady."

"Aye." She flexed her fingers against his chest and withdrew them abruptly. "Are we to travel far?"

"Six nights."

Far off, the howl of a wolf skipped over the hills and Katelyn pressed into him. Her trembling increased. His heart flexed.

"'Tis far off, dinnae be concerned," he assured her. He scowled when his voice came out gruff. That soft little body against his chest sent an increasing ripple of awareness through him. He threw his gaze up to the sky in a prayer for restraint.

"'Tis a clear night. We'll no' see rain," he offered weakly in an attempt to force his mind away from smooth flesh beneath thick fur.

"Aye."

He glanced down to see her gaze turn heavenwards. The

tilt of her lips reminded him of a plea to a lover.

For a kiss.

And for the briefest moment he considered dipping his head and brushing his lips over hers, just to see how they would feel. Finn clenched his jaw and looked away once more—away from temptation. This was another man's woman. And a vulnerable one at that. He did not need a helpless lass attaching herself to him.

A prickle skimmed along his side where their bodies touched. Ach, he was already too close. Any closer and he would be tucked beneath the fur and caressing that pale skin. He smirked to himself. At least keeping watch was going to be easy. In spite of the exertions of the day, sleep couldn't be further from his mind.

Noting her trembling had ceased, he drew in a long breath and focused on the pinpricks of light above him. It was a habit—staring at them and feeling insignificant. As a large man, there were few times in life when he felt like that. That gentle ache that always sat in his gut throbbed, reminding him of Alice's death—and the powerlessness that came along with that. Never again would he place himself in such a position.

That howl came again and he scowled. He hoped they were not being tracked though the fire was sure to keep the wolves at bay. Katelyn emitted a noise and he tightened his hold.

"They'll no' get close," he murmured, reassuring her again. Why did he feel the need to erase her fear? All that mattered was that he got her to his sister's keep. "We could see them coming many a mile away. We have been blessed with a bright night."

"Blessed..." she whispered, though he couldn't be sure if she intended for him to hear.

He supposed being taken from her home and dragged across the Highlands might not seem a blessing to her but it was surely a better fate than whatever that Norseman had planned for her.

"Aye, the heavens shine down upon us."

"I-I havenae seen a night like this in a while."

"'Tis beautiful indeed," he agreed and frowned at his words.

Sat on a lonely hill with the stars and an almost naked woman for company and here he spoke of beauty. It seemed he had little control over his tongue this night.

"The siege prevented me from going outside for many weeks." The hardened tone to her voice made his scowl deepen. She turned her face toward him, as if she expected a response and he fumbled in his mind for one. What did the lass wish of him? Was comfort not enough? Did she expect more of her rescuer? If he only understood women better.

Of course, if he'd been planning to bed her, he would have

done it with ease. But offering comfort or conversation... nay, he was far out of his depth here.

"But see now," he gestured to the sky, "the stars have come out for ye this night."

"For me?" The faintest hint of humour sat in her tone, a welcome relief from the frigidness.

"Aye, indeed. For ye, wee lass."

She softened a tiny bit more, truly moulding to him. "I have missed the stars."

"And they have missed ye. For who would not?"

Katelyn raised a quizzical brow and gazed up at him. "Ye are an unusual man."

"How so?"

"Ye speak softly of the stars, yet ye kill with ease."

"I do what I must."

She nodded slowly, her gaze turning back to the sky and he released a breath. "Aye, as do we all," she replied.

Something about that statement caught him. Did she speak of her betrothal perhaps? A noblewoman doing her duty was no strange thing. Indeed his sister had married the man of their father's choosing, but he'd never considered how a lass might feel about it. He had loved Alice, and she him. What would it have been like if neither of them cared for one another?

He flexed his fingers against Katelyn's delicate shoulder.

Less painful, for certain. Five summers and he no longer recalled Alice's voice or what her kisses felt like. For that, guilt jabbed at him. But the cries of pain as she tried to bring their daughter into the world—they echoed through his mind as if it were yesterday.

Soft breaths filtered in and he studied Katelyn's face in the starlight. She had fallen asleep. Her closed lashes against her swollen cheek eased the tension in his chest. He sighed. Soon enough, another man would be enjoying the sight.

***

Catriona awoke alone. She peered around. Nay, not alone, but no longer wrapped in the embrace of the Viking. Her muscles screamed in protest as she shuffled to sitting, fur clutched around her shoulders. The ache in her cheek seemed to have subsided at least. She glanced at the men. Still they slept on. She did not like her chances of evading all of them so surely now was the time.

A hand touched her shoulder and she swallowed a cry of surprise. Following the line of his body, silhouetted in the dawn light, she was confronted by a broad grin and broader shoulders.

Escaping *him*, however, would prove difficult.

"Did ye sleep well?"

Catriona fidgeted, aware of his gaze tracing her body. No

matter how she positioned herself, something peeked out of the pelt. A calf or her thigh. Even the curve of her shoulder, or the top of a breast. Interest sparked in his blue eyes, making her stomach flip.

She should be scared by him, not excited. Had she not already seen what a Norseman could do?

"Well enough, thank ye."

He knelt and handed over her gown. She gripped the wool in her free hand and offered Finn a tentative smile of thanks.

"'Tis dry now."

For some unknown reason, she failed to stop her smile from expanding at his obvious statement.

She stood, fighting to ignore how he followed her movements closely. "Will ye excuse me while I dress?"

His eyes crinkled at the corners, making her feel as though sprites might be dancing in her stomach. How did a barbaric Viking look so... so tender? She swept aside the notion she would miss the fair warrior. This was for the best. Whatever his plans for her, they could not be good.

"I shall turn my back," he offered.

Catriona nodded and motioned to an outcrop of rocks. "I will be but a moment." Furs clutched about her shoulders, she waited until he turned and scurried behind the rocks.

She fought the stiff fabric of her chemise and gown. Salt from the sea crusted upon it and the ties would be almost impossible to do on her own.

Once her chemise was on, she tugged the gown over her head and grimaced at the feel of the rigid garments against her skin. But at least she was no longer naked. She shook her head. Everything she had been taught about the Norsemen was wrong. Why had he not ravished her when given the chance? Did he not find her enticing? Catriona touched the swelling on her cheek. Mayhap the hit to her face had spoiled her looks. She never normally dwelled long on her appeal to men. It was an encumbrance and most thought her conceited when she dismissed them but, in truth, the attention made her uneasy. Katelyn and her father never understood why she did not use her looks to manipulate men, but she only concluded she had to take after her late mother, who knew little about plotting and scheming. Manipulation did not come naturally to Catriona.

So why did she care what her kidnapper thought? Sweet Mary, she really was turning into one of those women who fell in love with their abductor. She stretched her arms against the fabric to loosen it and *tutted* at herself. Not love, nay. She had not meant to say love. But certainly her feelings were far from fear. Which was a very foolish thing indeed.

Darting a peek over the grey rocks, she sighed as her gaze landed on the large man, his back still to her. The hills and valleys were all cast in muted colours, their splendour not yet allowed to shine through. If she travelled south she would come across one of the villages scattered across the countryside. In theory, returning to the coast would bring her close to civilisation but she was not sure she wished to risk such a venture. More Norse might have crossed from Bute by now.

A breeze glided across her back, reminding her of her gaping dress. There was little to be done. Without aid, tying it was impossible. Stealing one last glance at the magnificent Viking, she clutched her skirts and fled.

***

Tèile lifted her head from the rock and scrubbed her eyes. She blinked and scrubbed them again. Sure enough, the woman was scurrying off into the distance. Curses, what was she doing? One minute she'd been lying in Finn's arms and now the lass was disappearing off into the hills. She had felt sure a connection was already blossoming between the two. Why would the woman wish to run off alone, toward possible danger?

Wings spread, she gave them a flutter and wriggled. The

foolish man still had his back turned and had not realised she was gone. What was it with these Highland warriors? It seemed to Tèile these men and women spent half their time running from one another and fighting their feelings. Her life would be much easier if they said what they meant and got on with it. In spite of her time around humans, she still failed to fully understand them. If she did not like another faery, she told them. That was probably why the *sidhe* council took a disliking to her but still, it was surely better than keeping secrets?

The faery flew swiftly over to Finn and landed on his shoulder. She rolled her eyes. Humans did not see the fae unless they wanted to. Most were not able to even sense them but she could make him aware enough of her. With a smile, she jabbed one pointed finger at his neck. He made a sound of surprise and swatted, nearly crushing her with his huge hand.

Tèile scuttled back and tried again on the other side. This time she was ready and only felt the waft of air as he slapped the other side of his neck. She gritted her teeth in frustration. How long did he think it took for a woman to dress?

Snatching a small bunch of hair, she gave it a sharp tug and this time he swivelled. The scowl on his face gave way as realisation dawned. Off in the distance, Catriona could still be seen, stumbling over the rough land. Dawn began to make itself fully known, golden and pink hues streaking the sky. Her green dress might have blended with the hills but against the colourful backdrop, her silhouette stood out in stark contrast. Had they been further north and in rockier terrain, Catriona would have found it much easier to hide. Thank goodness for small mercies.

Finn snatched his sword and cursed. She hoped he had no plans to use the weapon but she noticed these warriors were strangely attached to such things. He kicked one of the men as he ran past and the man roused, grumbling. Flying alongside Finn, Tèile glanced behind to see him jump up and move to wake the others.

She turned her attention to their quarry. They would gain on her soon enough and Tèile could return to her work. If only she could figure out why the lass ran from Finn. It was hard enough trying to ensure fate fell back into alignment, but if Catriona fought it too long, it would make Tèile's job all the more difficult. Still, one thought made her smile. It only meant she would have to be extremely sneaky. And sneaky she could do.

***

Catriona glanced over her shoulder and her breath trapped in her chest. Hair streaming behind him, his sword in hand, the Viking looked every bit a powerful warrior intent on claiming his prize.

Her.

Quashing a squeal, she stumbled on. Every tiny rock and prickly plant seemed to find the soles of her feet. They were likely bleeding and raw. But she refused to stop. Not when her life depended on evading him.

The cumbersome gown grew heavy on her shoulders, no doubt weighted down by the dried salt from the sea water. Fatigue still lingered in her bones and the dull throb in her head nudged her, tempting her to stop and give herself up. However she had no doubt angered her abductor. While he had been patient and gentle with her before, who was to say if he would be kind now? Playing the meek captive might have worked to get him to trust her but she had destroyed that now. If he caught up with her, would she see the true nature of the man? Would the horrific tales she had been told come to life?

Her heart beat a sickening pace as she gulped down breaths of air. Dear Lord, but she was weary. How had she thought she could outrun such a physically capable man? Her ankle nearly buckled as she navigated the uneven path down the side of the hill and she swallowed a sob of desperation. A shout behind her sent a shiver up her spine but she continued on blindly.

Unaware how close he was until a rough hand curled around her wrist, she squealed as he jerked her to a halt. Both feet came out from beneath her and she toppled. Before the ground could greet her, powerful arms wrapped about her and dragged her to her feet. She fought and clawed against him, insensible sounds escaping. Frustration mingled with fear made her chest tight and breaths ragged. After the exertion of running, her vision grew fuzzy as drawing in air became more difficult.

"Cease, ye daft lass," he commanded roughly and hauled her up the brow of the hill.

His hold on her remained strong while he tried to pin her hands to both sides. She ended up entirely enveloped by him, unable to move let alone breathe.

"Pray…let me…go…" She pushed the words out against his chest.

The Viking's arms loosened marginally and she sucked in a deep breath. Tears dripped down her cheeks.

"What is this?" he asked gruffly. "Why do ye cry? Why do ye run? Lass, ye need not fear. Yer safe with me."

"How… how can I be safe with ye?" She peered up at him to see a flash of genuine hurt flicker across his face.

"I know ye have experienced things no lady should but surely ye know that I am not like that man. I wouldnae harm ye. I am here to protect ye."

"Protect me? How so?"

His brows almost knitted as he stared down at her. Something in his eyes reflected her own sense of vulnerability.

It forced her to relax. Powerful strokes of his hands across her back warmed her skin and soothed her racing pulse.

"I dinnae know how the attack has affected ye, Katelyn." His voice was low and as soothing as the palms on her gown. "But ye can be assured until we reach my sister's, no man shall touch ye."

"Ye… ye are touching me," she whispered. Then she scowled. "Yer sister's?"

"Aye, Lorna shall be sure to look after ye well. Until then, ye shall be under my care." His jaw tensed at the words.

Catriona blinked. "Why do ye take me to yer sister's?"

He drew back and skimmed a thumb over her head. "Ach, ye are more addled than I thought. Forgive me, lass, I—"

The dark haired man came up behind them and bent double to catch his breath. When he straightened, he slapped a hand to the man's shoulder.

"Finn…"

Catriona scowled at the man's name. She hadn't even known it. But Finn… that was no Viking name.

"What is it?"

"Norsemen… over the hill. They may be looking for the lass. Likely they travelled through the night."

"Damnation." Finn skimmed his gaze over her and slowly released her. "Will ye stay calm now, my lady? I wouldnae have ye run into the arms of the Vikings."

"The Vik—" Her legs trembled beneath her and she brought a hand to her mouth.

"Aye, they must have discovered yer absence. I suspect they would look to ransom ye, should they get hold of ye." He turned to the other man. "How many heads did ye count, Logan?"

Logan?

Another Highland name. Who were these men?

Catriona skipped her gaze from man to man, taking in their clothing, considering their behaviour.

"Some half a dozen, mayhap more."

"Ach, I like our odds but I dinnae want the lady caught in battle. What say ye, do we run or fight?"

Logan dipped his gaze to Catriona's bare feet. "I dinnae think we'll outrun them."

"Aye, ye may be right." Finn peered around and motioned to a nearby rocky outcrop with his sword. "My lady, ye must take shelter. Dinnae come out and dinnae be seen. We must see off these men if we are to take ye safely to Lorna's."

"Lorna... Lorna inghean Chaluim?"

Finn shook his head and eyed her again as if she had lost her mind. Mayhap she had. "Aye, lass. My sister. Go now, make haste."

Nodding, she snatched her skirts and scurried over to the rocks, pausing to stare at Finn. Lorna inghean Chaluim. She knew that name. Katelyn had been intending to stay with her before she married Laird Gillean mac Dhomhnaill. Sweet Lord, Finn was no Viking any more than she was. He had not captured her, he'd rescued her. These were the men who were meant to fetch Katelyn on Laird Gillean's behalf. No wonder she did not think him to be vicious and cruel like the man who attacked her.

His blue gaze latched onto hers briefly as the breeze ruffled his golden hair. His stark expression made her gut clench tight and something echoed between them across the open hills. Then he turned and ran. The other men had come up behind them quickly and they sprinted, swords drawn toward the encroaching attackers who, until now, were hidden behind the dip of the hill. Battle cries rang out and Catriona shuffled behind the rocks, gripping onto the cool stone, hoping to draw strength from it. If only she could cast her courage in stone—along with her heart. But her heart would not listen. It raced with fear for Finn and his men.

Her rescuer. How did she not see it? Yet he took her without a word dressed as a Viking. What else was she to believe?

Her thoughts scattered to the winds when she spotted the men clash. She ducked down briefly, closing her eyes to the savagery of battle, but a need to see Finn's fate drew her back up. The danger had not yet passed. He might still be killed. Or he could survive and discover her true identity. Then she might be cast aside when he learned the real Lady Katelyn was dead. And Gillean would turn his attentions to Bute once more. It was weak. Even if her father managed to retake the castle, until the King's men got there, they'd have little chance against Laird Gillean and his army.

A shudder wracked her and increased in intensity. Though far from her position, she heard the cries of men as they fought for their lives. Fought for *her* life. Her stomach churned when the crashing swords brought her back to the castle and the moment she thought she too would be a victim of war. Arms clenched around her waist, she battled to control the trembling of her body but it would not cease. Her hearing grew muted and all she saw was bloodshed. She watched each sword swing with horrified fascination.

Finn fought savagely, his size easily matching that of the Norsemen. He lunged and parried, striking down two men with little strain. When a gargantuan man faced him, Catriona's heart stuck in her throat. This man saved her and she had not even thanked him.

Whatever the future held for her, she at least hoped to be able to do that. His attacker took a large step forward and swung at Finn. He staggered from the blow and coldness gripped her, forcing a cry from her throat. The huge Norseman withdrew and raised his head toward her position. She clamped a hand over her mouth as he moved closer, his pace picking up—clearly realising who she was.

Or who she was meant to be.

Catriona scanned her surroundings, bile rising in her throat as the Viking drew nearer. His furs swung about, filthy hair trailed behind, and it felt as though the ground shook with his every footstep. She curled a hand about a loose rock and backed away, stone held aloft. By some miracle it did not slip from her clammy fingers.

Unable to keep her gaze from it, she stared at the bloodied tip of the attacker's sword. The blood of a highlander. She had not seen it, but he must have struck down one of the men. Would he strike her down too? Or mayhap he would pin her to the ground and start what the other man never finished? The trembling in her hands increased and the desire to run made her legs judder but she held firm. Finn's great courage gave her courage too. For these strangers who had shown her kindness, she must be brave.

The odour of the man reached her before he did. Just as he was to leap upon her, he darted sideways. The stone dropped from her fingers. She stared on as the Viking toppled to the ground. Only when he twisted did she realise Finn had tackled the man. They wrestled briefly but Finn easily matched his strength. With a blow from the hilt of his sword, he rendered him senseless, mayhap dead.

Catriona failed to summon any sympathy for the man. Only relief swam through her body, rendering her weak. She put a hand to the rocks for support. Finn clambered to his feet, a grin cracking his face, before turning to view the other Norsemen retreating. When he faced her, his smile dropped and he hurried to her side.

"Ach, yer white as a sheet and trembling like a leaf."

She bit her lip and nodded, not trusting her voice to work.

"I told ye we'd no' let ye come to harm, did I not?"

"Aye," she whispered.

He sheathed his sword and she forced herself not to contemplate the blood dripping from it. With one hand, he enveloped both of hers and held them still, and with the other he tilted her chin up.

Blazing blue eyes, that could not even compare to a clear sky seared into her. The touch of his rough hands warmed her—made her skin prickle. Another violent shudder and he dropped her hands to take her into his arms. Though not the first time he had held her, this time she did not think him her kidnapper. She sank into the embrace. Without even thinking, she flung her arms around his waist and buried her nose into his chest. No tears came, which surprised her. Only awful images of blood and terror played behind her eyelids. The scent of man and sea, a confusing mix of musk and salt mingled and she drew it in. Beneath her hands, she became aware of taut skin and muscle. Gradually, the world returned to her, mostly in the form of Finn. The scratch of his linen and plaid made her skin sensitive to his touch. One hand had come up to her hair, pinning her to his chest while the other smoothed over her back, just above her rear. Each sweep of his fingers sent a spiral of tension into her belly. Gone were the awful memories. Instead she pictured those fingers elsewhere. On her skin, her lips.

Catriona jerked, but only moved a little, as his hands still held her tight. What was she thinking? His fingers on her skin? She barely knew the man. And not a few moments ago, believed him to be a Viking. He offered her comfort, nothing more and yet she now swooned in his arms like some damsel.

She tugged back and this time he released her. Hands clamped in front, she licked her lips. "I thank ye, sir. I owe ye a great debt, it seems."

He flexed a hand and glanced at it, his brow furrowed. "Ye owe me naught. Save yer thanks for yer betrothed."

"Well, I offer my thanks regardless. Pray—"

Logan came to Finn's side, his features weary. "We've seen them off. With no losses either. Gerard took a swipe but 'tisnae deadly."

"Aye, thank ye, Logan," Finn replied distractedly, his gaze still firmly on her.

What she saw in that gaze, she could not be sure.

Confusion, it seemed, for even though he smiled, a line flexed between his brows as if unable to make her out. What confused him about her? Had he figured the truth? Surely not for there was no telling her and her sister apart. With their dark hair and gentle faces, only those who knew them well had ever been able to say who was who.

"Come then." He snapped his head away suddenly and laid a hand on Logan's shoulder. "Tend to Gerard and we must be on our way. Who is to say they will no' return with a larger force. It seems, my lady, that ye are a fine prize." His gaze flicked over her. "Fine indeed."

Catriona struggled to find a response. The way his voice lowered sent a curl of pleasure through her and her cheeks heated. Before any words came to her, he stomped off to check on his men. She regarded his back with a sigh. So broad and powerful. At least she knew she wasn't in danger of falling for her kidnapper. Nay, now it seemed she might fall for her hero instead.

CHAPTER THREE

With the fire lit and the men bedded down for the eve, Finn focused his attention on the lass. He tried not to question why he'd offered to take first watch again while knowing Katelyn did not yet sleep. The woman needed rest but she seemed unable to find it. She tossed and turned, the rustle of the furs the only sound for many miles. He plucked at the grass in front of him and lifted his head to the stars. No clouds followed them once again. The sky proved clear and pricks of light blanketed the heavens. He drew in a long breath and squeezed his hands together.

By God, he could not forget the feel of Katelyn's body beneath his palms. The slight curve of her rear had taunted him—nay—*begged* him to splay his fingers across it. Her sweet curves flattened against him made his body ache. He intended to offer comfort and instead he had startled her, mayhap even worse. What man took a woman in his arms after such an ordeal and considered stripping her bare and parting her thighs? Ach, but he disgusted himself.

He tore another chunk of grass from the ground and flung it into the night. He did not need to be thinking of such things. If only his dream lass returned to him. He'd not thought of her since meeting Katelyn. The woman in his imaginings might not be real but that did not matter to Finn. At least he did not have to fear for *her* safety. Katelyn had come too close to death once again today. Obviously these past days had planted much fear in her mind for her to consider running from him. He had failed her too many times now.

She muttered something and tossed again. Even though his mind begged him not to, his heart reached out to her. Coming to his feet, he edged his way over and sank down beside her. What a fool he was. His duty was to get her safely to Kilcree. He had no other obligations. So why did it pain him to see her restless and weary?

His admiration for her grew too. She had insisted on walking many miles barefoot. He had tried to persuade her to wear his boots, but they were too big and cumbersome. For some of the way, she'd allowed him to carry her. He enjoyed that far too much. A strong attachment to a lass was dangerous. The connection was too easily broken. He'd learned that once from his wife and he did not wish to repeat the experience.

Shaking away the memories, Finn touched her arm. She

rolled and gazed up at him. He had yet to decide on the colour of her eyes. In some lights they appeared green, in others, a darker shade more like that of a loch. He stared at her as if he could break through the night and study them once more. Why they had him so interested, he knew not. He surely had more important things to think on than her eyes.

"Ye cannae sleep?" he asked softly.

"Aye."

"Are ye cold?"

She shrugged. "A little."

"Shall I…" He coughed. "Shall I lie with ye for a wee while?"

Was it relief or disappointment that jabbed at him when she shook her head and pushed to sitting?

"Nay, but I would appreciate the company. I cannae seem to… my mind…"

"I understand."

"Have we far to travel? I have never visited Kilcree."

"Aye, some eighty miles. But our mounts await us at the next village. We shall travel the rest of the journey on horseback."

"And what… what does Lady Lorna expect of me, when we arrive?"

"Ye clearly dinnae know my sister. She wants for naught, save to ensure yer safety until the marriage arrangements are settled."

"I dinnae understand. I had no word of yer impending arrival. We thought we would receive a missive at least before ye arrived."

"Laird Gillean had word of the imminent attack and decided it best he bring forward his plans to wed ye."

"And pray tell why ye joined the rescue?" Katelyn drew her feet up and began massaging the soles of feet with her thumbs.

"Well ye will understand when ye meet Lorna that no man can say nay to her. Especially her brother."

"I must thank ye for yer kindness. Ye risked much."

"I confess we didnae expect to meet with an army of Norsemen."

She nodded slowly. "I am grateful ye at least arrived before..." She trailed off and even in the gloom, he saw her skin turn to ash.

In a bid to distract her, he settled in front and drew her feet onto his lap. "I should have allowed ye to tend to these sooner." He wrapped a hand around her ankle, ignoring the way it made the hair on his arms stand on end.

If he was not careful, those delicate toes in his lap might make something else stand to attention too. How could he find this woman so enticing when scarcely able to make out her features under her bruises?

Katelyn released a tiny sigh, barely audible, yet his hearing immediately latched onto it. Her lips moved as if trying to say something but nothing came. Instead she closed her eyes and leaned back on both hands while he rubbed her feet. Even in the gloom, he knew they were sore.

"Ye dinnae need to do that, sir."

"Ye may call me Finn, my lady."

"Finn," she whispered, sounding as if she was experimenting with the sound. "Ye may call me Cat—Katelyn."

"I cannae call ye Kat then?" he teased.

Instead of giggling as he expected, her eyes grew wide and she shook her head frantically. "N-nay. Katelyn if ye dinnae mind."

"I dinnae mind, Katelyn." Ach, why did his voice drop low as if her were seducing her?

Did she realise she had shifted closer? Her hand crept over to his forearm while her fingers drew circles on his arm, scalding him through the coarse linen of his shirt.

The delicate hand stilled as she peeked sideways at him. Ribbons of moonlight broke briefly through the clouds, sending a sparkle into her full lashed eyes. Regret, deep and bitter, pulled at his gut as it also highlighted the crimson swelling on her cheek.

A surge of protectiveness filled his chest. It was a sensation he hadn't felt in a long time. And he did not welcome it. It had been many seasons since he'd cared for the welfare of anyone but his kin. But he still had a duty to this woman so he would do what he must and ensure her safe arrival at Kilcree. If he could but force aside these invading thoughts, he would have no problem handling her with the same courtesy and teasing manner with which he always treated the lassies.

"Will we see the Norsemen again?" she asked quietly, breaking his thoughts.

"In truth, I dinnae know but dinnae fear. We have the strongest men my sister could offer."

"Yer sister was very kind to send ye. Ye risked much."

He offered a half shrug. "'Tis no matter. Ye are safe now and none were harmed."

In the dim light he saw her lashes drop, as if to conceal some emotion. He silently cursed his glib words. A delicate lady like Katelyn had no place amongst battle and had seen more than her fair share of atrocities.

"I am only sorry I didnae come sooner. Ye should never have experienced that brute's wrath."

A tiny shudder wracked her. He would not have made it out had he not been so close to her.

"In the midst of battle, some men are consumed by bloodlust. I cannae speak for my enemy but I would never allow my men to mistreat a lass, lady or no'."

"Aye," she agreed quietly.

"Alas, I dinnae think ye believe me yet, but I dinnae lay blame with ye. My barbaric ways didnae do much to recommend me. Ye must forgive me for frightening ye."

Her lashes lifted, her gaze glittered and he found himself staring at her, his fingers moving leisurely over her feet. Ach, when had he ever sat and stared into a woman's eyes? He was getting soft in the head in his old age. The only woman to ever draw his attention had been wee Alice. None could take her place and he did not wish them to. Aye, he was well enough on his own.

If only his body agreed. It had been too long. He simply needed a warm lass in his bed. A shivering, frightened, beaten woman was far from the perfect bed mate. If she had any idea of the heat that was amassing beneath his skin, she would think him no better than her attacker. Finn had never needed to force a woman to bed and he refused to have her think that of him.

In an effort to control himself, he retreated and released her foot. She made a tiny sound—like a noise of protest—but remained still. That puzzled him. Although her hand stroked his arm, seeking comfort, she did nothing else. After such a trial, would she not need reassurance from her rescuer?

Damnation, now what was he thinking? He did not want the lass in his arms, let alone regarding him as some magnificent hero. Still mayhap it rankled his ego that she had not swooned with gratitude. Most women he knew would take any chance to be in the arms of the fair haired warrior and protector of the clan at Glencolum.

The sound of a slight intake of breath dragged his attention back to Katelyn and he cursed himself again. This rescue had gone nothing like predicted. They were to go to the isle, take Katelyn with ease and place her in the hands of her betrothed.

Instead he had been embroiled in two battles, had a fragile yet strangely strong woman in his care and a Norse army searching for them.

"Ye should rest," he murmured to Katelyn when another yawn wrested free from her.

She shook her head. "I cannae."

"We have a long journey ahead of us. I will protect ye, have no fear."

"I dinnae fear for my safety, Finn. Ye seem a bold and brave warrior."

He grinned at her assessment of him. "Aye, bold indeed. Some would say too bold. It has brought me much trouble at times."

"Aye, but if ye hadnae been bold, I would probably be dead at the hands of that Viking."

His grin dropped. The thought of Katelyn—a woman he barely knew—coming to harm made his gut clench. When the rush of bloodlust had dimmed, he had no doubt the image of her attacker attempting to rut against her would linger.

Katelyn touched his chin, the lightest of touches that sent an odd tingling sensation through him. He forced a smile again. How odd that even in the dark night she could make out his mood. Few people saw past his ready smiles and teasing wit.

"I am very grateful to ye."

"Ye may save yer gratitude, Katelyn, for yer betrothed." He didn't know why, but he needed to remind her of Laird Gillean. Or was he reminding himself?

"I shall surely thank him too, but it was ye who took the risk of dressing as one of the enemy and infiltrating the keep mid-battle."

"Ach, 'twas no huge risk. I've been mistaken for a Viking many a time."

"Aye…"

She sighed and tilted her head up toward the heavens. The moonlight that invaded the sky shone brightly enough to allow him to make out her profile. He swallowed. He had not noticed her true beauty until then but with her dark hair streaming down her back, even with the swelling on her cheek, he surely had a handsome woman beside him.

Ach, moonlight and a beautiful woman. Fate was playing a cruel trick indeed on him.

***

Finn pressed a coin into the hand of the villager who had stabled their mounts for their journey. There had been nowhere to leave them by the coast and knowing of their need to cross the sea, Finn had made the decision to stable their horses in the village.

He rubbed a hand down Dìleas's flank and grinned. "Ye look well, lass. I think ye've been enjoying yer break too much. Ye shall have to ride hard now."

"This is yer horse?" Katelyn's asked as she approached from behind.

"Aye, this is Dìleas—my faithful companion. She shall see us safely to Kilcree."

Katelyn blinked. "I shall ride with ye?"

"Aye, we didnae bring an extra mount. Dinnae fear, she is a strong horse and can easily bear the burden."

Her throat bobbed lightly. What disconcerted her? The thought of riding with him? Mayhap it was the impropriety of their situation but it could not be helped. He had to admit the idea of having her pressed up against him sent a thrill through him in spite of himself.

Mounting the brown horse, he offered her a hand and settled her up behind him with ease. She released a tiny gasp as he lifted her and the sound made him clench the reins hard.

They set off at a steady pace, wary of tiring out the horses. Passing by the ramshackle cottages, smoke seeping from their straw roofs, Katelyn wriggled to get comfortable. Her slender legs rubbed his thighs and her fingers touched tentatively at his waist. Dìleas wandered to one side slightly, struggling against her added—*wriggling*—burden. By his reckoning, this journey would be a long, long one.

"Ye have a fine steed, Finn." Katelyn lifted her voice over the steady beat of hooves.

"Aye, she is indeed fine."

"Ye have had her long?"

"Aye, some ten years."

"Was she yer father's?"

Finn scowled. He'd forgotten how much women like to talk. When he spent time with lasses, it was rarely for conversation. He shoved aside one idea he had for keeping her quiet. Placing his mouth over her lips and—damnation. "Nay, my father died many years ago."

"Forgive me."

"'Twas a while ago and I have many kin around me," he replied stiffly. His father had died of a battle wound—an honourable death, everyone assured him.

"And yer mother?"

"Aye, dead too." Sickness had taken her several years after his father's death. Yet another lass taken from him by some unseen enemy.

"As is mine."

"I am sorry."

"'Twas long ago too. But I do miss her." He felt her sigh against his back. "Ye have other brothers and sisters?"

"Nay, just Lorna. But she is enough for any brother to handle." Her hand dropped and grazed the top of his thigh and he coughed. "And ye?"

"I had—have a twin sister," she mumbled.

Interesting. He hadn't heard mention of another sister. No wonder the lass was traumatised, having been torn apart from a close sibling. "A twin? Why were ye no' with her?"

"I—we're not close. She was likely with my father."

"Well then, I am sure she is well." He reached behind and squeezed her fingers, regretting it immediately when those soft tips settled in his palm.

Dìleas jerked on the reins as Katelyn shifted again and Finn muttered a soft oath. On such uneven ground, he risked the mount injuring herself.

"Is something amiss?" he asked more sharply than intended.

She yanked her fingers from his. "Nay," she replied huskily.

He gripped the leather bridle and nudged the horse back on course. Dìleas could cope with much but Katelyn's discomfort was putting her on edge. And him. He tried not to miss her delicate fingers in his hand.

Dìleas tensed beneath him. If only the lass would relax.

"If ye are tired ye can rest against me."

"I am no' tired."

He masked a snort. "And I suppose yer feet dinnae hurt either. Mayhap I should have ye walk the rest of the way," he teased.

Silence reigned and Finn cursed inwardly. He'd hoped to draw her out of her unease, not create further tension. And his natural reaction was to jest. She softened as did the horse and he released the air from his lungs.

"I dinnae believe ye would make me," she responded, a smile in her voice.

The sound warmed his heart. He longed to turn and see that smile. "I might be persuaded to."

"After all the effort to bring me from Bute, you would discard me so easily?" A hand curled around his upper arm.

"Indeed. I might even put ye back on the boat and have ye row yerself back."

She gasped. "And here I had ye marked as an honourable man."

Honourable? Would she still think that if she knew of all the heated thoughts he kept having? He longed for—and dreaded—the moment fatigue would overcome her and those luscious breasts ended up pressed against his back.

He needed to create some distance. "Alas, I am naught but a humble warrior."

"That I dinnae believe for a moment."

"What? That I am no' humble?"

She laughed. "Nay, that ye are naught but humble. But I would question that too, now you speak of it."

"Ach, I dinnae know what I have done to be so harshly judged." He grinned. Her laughter danced in his ears, a low and sensual sound. The kind of laugh a lover might hear if he skimmed his lips over her skin.

This time it was his nervous movements that had Dìleas tensing beneath him. He forced himself to relax.

He heard her yawn and his grin stretched. Stubborn lass. The wee woman was certainly made of strong stuff.

"Rest against me," he commanded gently.

"Nay, I told ye, I am no' tired."

"Yer disconcerting Dìleas."

"Oh."

"I willnae bite." *Hard*, he added silently, then mentally kicked himself.

"I know." That smile flowed through her voice again.

First one hand, then the other curled tighter around him. He ground his teeth together. Then came her cheek as she leaned into him. Next her breasts. He lifted his gaze to the skies and prayed for restraint. Through his plaid and her gown, that rounded flesh scorched him.

Hell fire, he would need more than prayers and his sword arm to see him through this journey.

***

After a day's riding, Catriona sank gratefully to the ground and stretched out her legs by the narrow stream that slipped between the rocks. She dipped her toes into the icy water, gasping when it bit into her skin. She sighed and listened to the soothing trickle as she got used to the temperature. It numbed the scratches and eased the aches. She tilted her head back and drew in a long breath.

"Drink, lass."

She jolted when Finn appeared at her side and sat upright, guilty that he caught her in a vulnerable moment. She'd tried hard not to complain about their journey. Not only had these men risked their lives for her, but they'd risked their lives for the wrong woman.

He offered the leather skin again and she grasped it and smiled her thanks. She had little appetite or thirst but she needed to keep up her strength if she was to survive the coming days. Her body ached from a day's riding. Ensuring some distance remained between her and Finn made her arms hurt. Eventually she gave in and rested upon his back, but tension riddled her thighs from so long in the saddle.

Already, she had nearly let slip the truth behind her identity. It took much concentration to remember she was meant to be her sister. She glanced at the fair warrior as he eased off his boots and stepped into the stream. Finn bent, scooped a handful of water and scrubbed his face before doing the same with his hair. Rivulets of water skipped down his throat and she watched their journey until they disappeared under his shirt. His hair, darkened by the water, rested over his shoulders, dampening the linen. A small braid behind his ear, bound by leather, begged to be played with.

Catriona dropped her gaze as he caught her eye and smiled, but there was no fighting it. His strong jaw, graced with stubble, a slightly long nose and intense blue eyes all drew her attention. On his bottom lip, a small scar caused her fingers to tingle as the odd urge to trace it teased her. She watched him, unable to tear her gaze away, and prayed he did not think her strange.

She should not be thinking it—not after what she had been through—but the man had somehow charmed her. No doubt a man like Finn found it easy to charm the lasses, but why had she succumbed so easily? If she allowed her thoughtsto dwell on the previous days' events, a well of terror would threaten to break through her restraint, and yet around

Finn she felt safe and at ease.

"Drink then, lass."

Catriona blinked and stared briefly at the flask in her hands. Ach, but she must appear a fool. Taking a quick drink, she gasped as fiery liquid—and not ale as expected—burned down her throat and simmered in her stomach.

"'Tis mead?" she asked breathily.

"Aye. Good for keeping ye warm."

She nodded. The mead worked quickly into her muscles, making them loose and the heat flowed through her. Now she was expecting it, she took another swig and savoured the sensation, but when she went to take another drink, Finn tapped her shoulder.

"We just want ye warm, Katie. Not senseless," he teased.

Catriona couldn't resist returning his smile. "I shouldnae drink any more anyway. I shall fall asleep if I am no' careful."

"Aye, it has been a hard day's riding." He made a show of stretching and wincing.

She raised a brow. "Ye tease me? I dinnae believe ye found today hard at all."

He shrugged and gave her a bashful look, one that told her he had been trying to make her feel better. "I ache a little."

"Ach!" She laughed and his returning chuckle set butterflies alight in her stomach.

"Ye'll forgive me that I cannae leave ye alone to bathe.

Ye'll have to settle for a light wash."

Warmth bloomed in her cheeks. In her mind those large hands and blunt fingers were upon her, peeling away her gown and scrubbing away the grime and fatigue. Then those fingers grazed hers as he took the flask and helped her to her feet. If she glanced down would her whole body be aflame? Because that was surely how she felt. Even the bitterly cold steam failed to cool the heat within her.

They stood for a moment. Their gazes connected brashly and even embarrassment couldn't make her look away. What did he see? She hadn't even been able to see her reflection in the bubbling water of the stream. Did any of her beauty shine through her bruises and grimy skin? And why did she care?

Flustered, she tugged her hand away and scooped up some water, bringing it up to her face. The water cooled her heated skin and gave her a moment to steady herself. Finn likely saw her as nothing more than a woman under his protection. A man doing his duty. Not to mention he thought her someone else. A day flattened against his back, feeling the undulation of his muscles did nothing to help her make sense of her situation.

Aware of Finn standing close enough for her to touch, Catriona kept her gaze on the shiny grey rocks while she dipped to scrub her feet and calves. Her gown skimmed the water but it mattered little. Already stained and filthy, a little damp would do no harm.

Smears of blood—the Viking's blood—painted the forest green wool of her gown, drawing her attention as she snatched her skirts. Clutching the fabric until her hands ached, she willed the memories to disappear. But they would not. She could almost feel his sweaty hands upon her, smell his acrid breath and remember the pounding horror that had her convinced she was to die.

Someone put a hand to her shoulder and she squeaked as crimson liquid spilled across her in her mind. With a heavy swallow, she met Finn's concerned gaze. He watched her intently. How much did he see? The thought that mayhap he had figured her out made her stiffen.

"Dinnae be afeared. I'll no' let anything happen to ye."

She drew up her chin. That Viking's actions and grisly death would not defeat her. Somehow she was determined to overcome it and forget such scenes.

"I am no' afeared," she told Finn. His eyebrows darted up—surprised, she assumed. It emboldened her. That she shocked such an obviously worldly man made her lips twitch.

"I could take the first watch if ye wish."

Finn shook his head, barely smothering a laugh. "Nay, lass, ye just rest. We've men enough to deal with anything that may come our way. Ye'd do better gathering yer strength for the rest of the ride." He paused and pinned her down with a knowing look. "Ye've had a trying day."

Curse the man. How did he see so easily through her? Her false bravado lent her a sense of security yet he stripped it away with one glance. They fell silent, only the wind sighing between the valleys accompanying the pounding of her heart in her head.

Unable to bear his scrutiny any longer, Catriona grabbed her skirts and stepped toward the grass. A sharp stone jabbed her foot and she cried out as she lost her footing. Solid hands came around her waist, enclosed her in a shield of masculinity and stopped her from slipping. Her hands fell onto his forearms as she steadied herself. His skin pulsed beneath her fingertips. Coarse fair hair begged her to run her palms up and down his arms.

She stared at Finn's arms for a moment—or mayhap longer. Time drifted and an awareness of his palms pressed above her hips seeped in, made her breathless. When she finally lifted her head, his blue eyes had darkened, his grin absent. With a sudden movement, he tugged her into him, hand splayed over the base of her spine, the other crushing her hair. Breasts pressed against his chest, her nipples peaked.

His gaze dropped to her lips and she knew what was coming. Lips parted, she fought to draw a breath as he dipped his head. Her lids fluttered closed even while her mind told her to flee, to break from his hold.

"Damnation."

The warmth of his body left her and she flicked open her eyes, blinking at the sight of Finn stumbling up onto the grass and falling into a sprint. When she had steadied herself, she realised one of the horses was galloping down the hill to the bottom of the valley. Something must have startled it. Taking a shaky breath, she dipped her fingers in the water and blotted it across her chest in a bid to cool her skin.

Sweet Mary, how close she had been to kissing him. What was wrong with her? She had never been interested in men. Catriona stepped out of the stream, the grass tickling her cold feet and pressed her fingers to her lips. She watched as Finn caught up with the horse and mounted her with ease. He offered her a jaunty smile and her heart leaped.

She could ill afford to fall for Finn, not when she had to keep up this ruse. Hopefully her father would find out where she was and send for her soon enough and it would all be over.

He galloped past her to where the men were setting up camp for the night and she let slip a reluctant smile. Running a hand through her tangled hair, she shook her head, willing to bet many a night she would wonder what it might have been like had Finn kissed her.

***

Smoke drifted up into the air and disappeared against the inky sky. The low murmur between the men was only punctuated by the occasional pop of wood. Tèile satisfied herself with resting between the fire and Catriona. She dare not sleep too close to the flames or an errant spark might strike her and her wings would go up in flame in no time. She shuddered. Trapped here with no wings...

If only these humans appreciated the sacrifice she was making for their happiness.

Glancing at the highlander sitting on the slight rise of a slope, she shook her head. He watched over their encampment, but Tèile saw his gaze tracking to where Catriona slept. They'd both avoided one another after that near kiss. That had been far too close. If they acted on their attraction too soon, fate would still be out of alignment. Curses. It was such a fine line. The smallest of action could throw so much out of balance—as she had learned the hard way. She hadn't even had to consider her actions when it came to Morgann and Alana.

Thank goodness that horse responded to her request so quickly and distracted them. Tèile propped her chin on a hand. At least she'd have no problems bringing them together when the time came. When they realised their love for one another— *at the right time*—all would be well once more and she could return home. Finally.

***

The final day's ride to Lorna's keep proved to be quick and easy. The start of summer treated them to clear skies and the worn paths snaking through the valleys were dry. They made good time, only stopping briefly to rest. The gentle skim of Katelyn's fingers on Finn's waist, occasionally brushing the top of his thighs brought him more pleasure than it should have. And more discomfort.

When the tall walls of Kilcree keep came into sight, he sighed and patted his mount encouragingly. Men milled around the wall that surrounded the large keep. Moss clung to the square towers, painting the grey stone green in places and Finn knew that was down to the old laird's neglect. Lorna had been very determined to ensure Kilcree Castle be restored to its former glory upon the death of her husband two summers ago. Soon the keep would be something to be admired once more if Lorna had anything to do with it.

Several men-at-arms recognised him when he navigated his horse between the gap in the wall and toward the stables. The small building sat apart from the keep and he found himself slowing, as if to put off the inevitable.

Soon he would say farewell to Lady Katelyn.

Which would be no bad thing, he reminded himself. Though they had maintained a courteous relationship, tension simmered in the air between them. All because of that near kiss. Every time he considered it he had the desire to punch something. What a fool, trying to kiss the lass he was to deliver to her betrothed. He couldn't decide if Katelyn's attitude toward him was born of embarrassment or because she too wished to kiss him. He caught her looking at him sometimes and in those moments he convinced himself that she needed to taste his lips just as much.

He dismounted, adjusted his sword on his belt and helped Katelyn down. Colour sat high on the cheek not marred by bruises and he stared at her for a moment. Those green eyes drew him in and under his hands her breaths quickened, her ribs expanding against his palms. A stable hand scurried over as the other men brought their horses in and they broke apart hurriedly. Katelyn murmured her thanks and backed away as Finn saw Dìleas into a stall.

Drawing a breath, he took a moment to pet the horse's muzzle. All he had to do was hand over Katelyn to Lorna. That was it. Then he could be on his way. So why did the thought of leaving the lass create a knot in his throat?

A careful grin across his face, he stepped out of the stall and offered his hand to Katelyn. She nodded her appreciation and laid her hand across his. The touch of delicate fingers sent warmth to his groin. Many times on their journey he'd held his breath and prayed for those fingers to inch further down. He shook his head and led her up the few stone steps to the keep. Her grip tightened and when he glanced at her, he noted her stiff spine and tense expression. Something made the lass nervous. He gave her fingers a tiny squeeze and pushed open the heavy wooden doors. The slight smile she rewarded him with made his heart skip.

Rosemary and lavender drifted through the air when they stepped in, mingled with the smoke of the fire pit in the centre of the room. While the weather was warming, the stone of the keep held in the cold. It pleased him to note the Great Hall looked well-tended, as did his sister. The years he'd spent dealing with the problems in Glencolum and leaving his sister in the hands of Logan and her late husband did not play on his mind so much when he saw how well she handled things on

her own.

His fair haired sister turned and her eyes widened when she spotted Katelyn and then her gaze fell on something behind him. He peered over his shoulder at Logan, whose brow dipped into a frown. He nodded his acknowledgement to Lorna and hastily made his way up the inner stairs to the balcony. Finn scowled and watched his sister carefully as he approached. Lorna had always been close to Logan, so why the cold reception?

At four and twenty—some three summers younger than him—she remained youthful looking though the sweet shape of her face belied her determination and sometimes disagreeable temper. Not that he'd have her any other way, but not many men liked a woman who spoke up readily.

"Well, sister, have ye no embrace for me?"

She laughed, her frown quickly gone and snatched her skirts to scurry over. Wrapping her arms about him, she squeezed his waist before pulling away. "I am pleased to see ye safe." She took Katelyn's hands and smiled warmly. "And ye, Katelyn. I feared greatly for ye. It seems my brother didnae take as good a care of ye as I'd hoped." A teasing glint lit Lorna's eyes but she had to know how much it galled him that Katelyn had been harmed.

Katelyn withdrew her hands and touched her bruised cheek. "Oh, nay, yer brother did all he could. He risked a great deal to come to my aid."

"Well, I am only sorry we didnae come sooner. None expected the Norsemen to cross so soon."

"It took us by surprise too."

A heartbeat passed and Finn tapped his foot.

Katelyn, ye must be weary," Lorna finally said as she signalled to a serving maid who came scurrying over. "Mae, have Lady Katelyn seen to her chambers and fill a bath."

This brought out a relieved smile from Katelyn. "I thank ye, my lady."

"Pray call me Lorna. We shall speak more on these sorry events later. First ye must bathe and rest."

Something akin to apprehension flickered across Katelyn's face but it faded quickly and she dipped her head briefly. "Thank ye, Lorna," she said softly.

They watched her follow the maidservant up the wooden stairs to the balcony. Finn forced his gaze away from the gently swaying curves under her gown. Ach, even in filthy torn garments she tempted him. Dragging his head around, he focused on his sister. "All is well then?"

"Aye, as ye can see, Finn." Lorna motioned around.

He scanned the Great Hall, noting she was right. He'd only briefly stopped by on the way to Bute but on his previous visits, the red tapestry—a depiction of a great battle—had been threadbare and dusty, the chandeliers looked in need of a clean and the rushes on the floor had likely not been replaced for many summers. Now it looked as though his sister had commissioned a new trestle table for the rear of the hall and the wooden railing surrounding the gallery that spanned the entire length of the hall looked to be new too.

"All looks well indeed. Though Logan didnae look so happy."

"Ach, the man simply cannae handle a lass telling him what to do."

He fixed Lorna with a stare. She kept something from him.. "That doesnae sound like Logan. He normally bows to yer every will," he observed.

"Well not this day, he does not." Tugging her skirt, she glanced down before meeting his gaze once more. "What are yer plans then, Finn? Shall ye return to Glencolum?"

"Ye have tired of me already, sister?"

She shook her head and grinned. "Tell me, did all go well?"

Finn sighed, retreated to the table at the rear of the hall and poured himself an ale. Draining it in one long drink, he placed the goblet down and swiped the back of a hand across his mouth. He fixed Lorna with a stare. "We arrived as the Norse were breaking through the walls."

A hand went to Lorna's mouth. "Sweet Lord, I didnae expect ye to have to go in amidst the battle."

"Aye, 'twas fierce at that. But," he grinned at the memory, "yer brother wouldnae fail ye so I killed the nearest Viking and disguised myself. Aside from a small scuffle, it worked."

Lorna let slip a smile. "A fine idea, brother. Ye'd make a good Norseman by my reckoning."

"Well ye didnae get all the wit in the family, Lorna."

"So ye rescued Katelyn without incident?"

Terrified green eyes and a trembling body played in his mind. "Almost. Lady Katelyn was set upon before I could get to her."

"Poor lass..." she breathed.

Finn strolled around the trestle table and drew out one

of the large chairs behind it, the one that used to seat Lorna's husband. He trailed his fingers across the wood carvings before sitting. Weariness suddenly ate into his limbs. "But still, she has ye now."

"For now. Laird Gillean will be here soon and will wed her here so that she may travel to his home as his wife and without a chaperone."

"Aye," he replied quietly.

"Ye know Gillean has threatened war upon Katelyn's clan. This marriage was to be a peace treaty."

"In truth?" He snorted. "He is too late though. War is upon Bute already."

"It matters little to Gillean. The isle will be back in Katelyn's father's hands before long and Gillean is land hungry. He knows Bute is weak and 'twill be even more so once the Norse are driven from it." She swiped a hand across the table. "And then no doubt, he will turn his attention to my lack of a husband." She laughed but Finn did not miss the tension in it.

"He shall find ye a good man, surely? He would not want his castle in the hands of a fool."

"Gillean's notion of a good man and my own differ greatly I fear, but alas, if I want to keep my home, I shall have to bow to the will of my overlord." Lorna sighed. "Such is the lot of a woman," she added drolly.

"Ye know ye always have a place at Glencolum should ye need it. Morgann and I will protect ye from aught should ye need us."

A soft smile slipped across her face and she patted his hand. "I thank ye, Finn. Ye are a noble man. But I have survived worse and I shall survive again."

Finn forced down the knot in his throat. He knew little of Lorna's marriage. She had been sold into it at six and ten before their father died. Her husband was an old man but a good warrior. Likely there was no love between them, but how many marriages were made of love in times of war and politics? Still the churning of his stomach told him there was more to Lorna's marriage than she let slip. And that gnawing sensation also said he'd failed her by not being a better brother to her during it. If only the cursed fighting at Glencolum had not taken such a toll.

He coughed. "Forgive me, sister, I—"

She waved her hand. "All is well now. I shall not worry until Gillean arrives and in the meantime I shall occupy myself with caring for our new guest. No doubt she has endured much."

"Lorna, ye are so very fond of taking in strays."

"Ach, ye are soft-hearted too, Finn. Ye keep it hidden beneath yer quick grin and rakish ways."

"First, Logan, now Katelyn."

"Logan was no stray." Her brows dipped and she drew her chin up.

He fought the urge to chuckle. Something about Logan riled Lorna. "Nay, he was but a peasant boy, was he not?"

"Finn, dinnae talk of him that way. Ye fight beside him and know well enough he is more than that. Ach, ye could learn some lessons from him. At least he knows how to behave as a gentleman."

He snatched the goblet and poured himself more ale, using the earthenware to disguise his grin. So righteous. Lorna loved to jump to the defence of anyone whom she felt needed her. Logan had been nothing but a poor man when he'd come to Kilcree looking for work. And while there might be no noble blood in him, Finn had to admit, he knew few men who fought as well as Logan.

"So," he traced the wood grain of the table with his free hand, "when are we expecting Katelyn's marriage to take place?"

"Gillean travels from the south on business. I think it likely we shall not see him for at least two sennights."

"Would ye object to yer brother staying for a while?"

"Ye know I wouldnae, but does Morgann not need ye?"

"Ach, Alana has him in hand. My duties have lessened vastly of late." Indeed, his responsibilities at Glencolum had decreased since the fighting with Alana's clan had ended and the lass took to running the castle with ease. It left him with too much time. Time to think on the past, on his future....

Lorna smiled and leaned over, pressing a hand to his forearm. "Finn, ye are the best kind of a brother."

He shifted. "If I were the best kind of brother, I would have been here more often."

"Ye had much to deal with at Glencolum. The fighting took up much of yer time. I am only grateful ye were never harmed. Of course, losing Ali...."

He stood abruptly, his heart wringing at the mention of his wife. "'Tis settled then. I shall extend my stay."

She blinked at the sudden interruption but gathered herself, squeezing her hands together. "I am sure I can tolerate ye just a wee bit longer, but I fear ye shall find yerself tired of the slow pace of life here. There are no battles for ye to fight."

"Nay, and for that ye should be grateful."

Aye, the more he thought on it, the more convinced he became he should stay a while longer. He'd already spent too much time away from his sister and he perceived trouble in her eyes—something to do with Logan mayhap. An undercurrent of *something* fizzled through the air. He contemplated the jug of ale in front of him. Of course, his decision to stay had little to do with Katelyn. Her fate was of no consequence to him.

CHAPTER FOUR

Catriona blew the soapy bubbles from her hands and leaned back in the wooden tub with a sigh. Warm water caressed her skin and removed much of the fatigue and aches from her body. But while her muscles eased, her stomach churned with worry. What had she done? Lorna appeared as kindly as Finn had suggested.

She released a breath. Deceiving either of them rankled. Finn had been so kind and courageous. She shut her eyes. Fair hair and deep blue eyes lingered in her vision behind her closed lids. Catriona clenched her hands together until nails dug into her palms. Why did Finn make her tense again? Being attracted to him only further complicated things. And besides, he would be gone soon.

At least that put one problem behind her. Even if it made her heart ache a wee bit. She had to remember why she was continuing this deception. It was not for her father, nay, but for the people of Bute. The Norsemen would be expelled from the isle and it would be vulnerable to Laird Gillean's advances. It had to appear that her father at least wanted to continue with the contract. Both she and her sister had large dowries but even to offer herself as a replacement would be seen as breaking the contract and might tear apart their tentative peace. Not that she wished to be sold to the laird. Likely her father never intended to go through with the agreement anyway. He had much higher ambitions for his daughters.

Alas, his perfect daughter was dead and now he was left with her. Still she might not want power and money as Katelyn had but she would prove her worth in this matter at least. She would prevent war and save her people from further distress. That, at least, she could do right.

She scrubbed her arms, plucked the soap from where it had sunk, lathered up some more bubbles and set to work on her legs. She froze as she spied the bruises on her inner thighs. Her mouth grew dry and the rose scent lingering in the air seemed to become tinged with sweat and blood. The soap slid from her trembling hands and she splashed water over her face as if it would remove the memory of the Viking's hands on her. When it still refused to leave, she submerged herself under the water and held herself there for a few moments.

When she broke through the surface, Catriona drew in great breaths and concentrated on calming her racing heart. Gaze fixed on the daylight seeping through the partially closed shutters, she clamped her hands by her side. Even being in a place of safety failed to remove her fears. How was it she felt more safe and secure in Finn's embrace than in a heavily guarded castle?

The thud in her chest slowed and she continued to suck in steady breaths. How she would overcome this, she knew not, but she had to keep hold of her senses. In such a precarious position, one slip and all could come crumbling down. She shook her head and dragged her hands through her hair. So many uncertainties. So much at stake.

***

Having consumed enough ale to warm his aching limbs, Finn stood beneath the large tapestry on one wall and admired it. "Ye have done a fine job," he said to Lorna. "But do ye nae think ye should turn yer attentions to—" Finn trailed off as a woman descended the stairs from the upper gallery, footsteps so soft he barely heard them.

He let his gaze linger slowly on her and watched the slight sway of her hips beneath her purple gown. The thud of his heart was almost sickening in its rhythm and his temples throbbed as blood surged through his body.

"By God..." he caught himself whispering when she reached the bottom step and lifted her gaze to his.

Her beauty stole his breath. It was a cool beauty but

one of utter perfection. Long, black hair draped over her shoulders in waves that begged to be touched. With the front strands tied back, he had a perfect view of her faultlessly oval shaped face and succulent lips. She hung back, hands clasped tightly in front as if waiting permission to approach but he still noted the divine shape of her lips, the little dip at the top of them. The sort of lips capable of bringing a man to his knees.

The woman from his dreams.

Katelyn was the woman from his dreams. How was it possible and how had he not realised?

Lorna coughed and he jolted, reluctantly dragging his gaze from Katelyn.

The woman in question cautiously approached and Finn dipped his head briefly, spreading a warm grin across his face. Mayhap he disconcerted her as her eyes widened. He almost laughed. He was used to women instantly simpering under such a look but she seemed to view him as if he were a wolf on the prowl.

He had to admit he felt like one. Never before had he seen a woman so spectacular. Even his dreams did her no justice. And to think he had laid next to her with nothing more than a fur between them. How had he not recognised it was she?

"Ye look very well, Katelyn." He murmured her name and savoured how it rolled on his tongue.

A blush of colour blossomed across her pale cheeks as

she inclined her head toward him slowly. "Thank ye, sir. The yarrow root Lorna gave me has done much for my injuries." A hint of a smile teased her lips. "And a bath does much for a woman's health."

"Finn," he corrected, longing to hear her husky tones utter his name and disappointed by her sudden formality.

"Finn."

It was as if she had to force the word from her mouth but he almost closed his eyes and groaned as she spoke. Finn took the chance to admire her up close. In a gown of purple silk, she looked resplendent... and far too tempting. Rounded breasts shaped her gown and his palms tingled while he imagined how perfectly they would fill his hands. The swelling on her cheek had all but gone and even the faint bruising could not detract from her beauty.

Katelyn rung her hands and darted her gaze between him and his sister. Dare he hope she was thinking the same? The ache in his body grew and Katelyn was most certainly the source. Finn longed to put a permanent smile on her face. He couldn't help wonder if a dose of unrestrained loving may well prove to be the best way of doing it. Which was pure folly. She would be in the bed of another man before long.

Her betrothed. Why did he find it so hard to remember that?

Lorna jabbed an elbow lightly in his side and he realised

he must have been staring.

"Are ye feeling revived?" Lorna asked.

"Aye, much better, thank ye."

"Should ye like a tour around? Laird Gillean shall not be with us for several sennights by my reckoning, so this shall be yer home for a while yet."

"I see." Katelyn's voice came out barely more than a whisper, making Finn scowl. She showed little excitement at the idea of meeting her betrothed.

"Ah, Logan." Lorna motioned to the brooding man as he entered the hall, a glower on his face. Finn resisted the urge to chuckle. The man had been out of sorts ever since their return. His sister had something to do with his dour mood, he suspected. "Will ye show Lady Katelyn around the keep and lands? I have a need to speak with Finn."

Finn fought the desire to mimic Logan's scowl as a dart of disappointment jabbed him. *He* wanted to show Katelyn around. In spite of himself, just being without Katelyn caused a strange ache in his chest. He'd already experienced it when she went to her chambers to wash and rest. Those few days traveling together—those few *short* days—reminded him of what it was like to have a woman for company. He rubbed a hand over the back of his neck and glanced at his sister's all too serious expression. It was a reminder he did not need or want.

"If ye'll come with me, my lady," Logan dipped his head

to Lorna before turning away.

"I thank ye. Good day to ye." Katelyn curtseyed and turned to depart, but not before throwing a lingering glance at Finn. Wariness and uncertainty haunted those stunning eyes. Did the previous days' events cause such a look or was it something more? He couldn't help but wonder and wish he knew more.

"Will ye tell me more of what happened on Bute?"

Finn snapped his attention to Lorna. "I cannae tell ye much, save that the Norsemen succeeded in capturing the castle."

"What of Katelyn's father?"

"I wasnae there long enough to meet with the laird. My priority was Katelyn, as dictated by yer husband's brother," he responded stiffly. He would not have a lass tell him he hadn't done his duty, sister or not.

"'Twill be a while until we hear word from Bute and of the outcome of the siege," she mused.

"The king will send men over to take it back, will he not?"

"I know not. If the laird lives, he may be expected to fight the Norse himself."

"If he lives."

"Which is my concern. Katelyn has not only lost her home but may have lost her father too."

"Ye show a great deal of interest in that woman, Lorna."

"As do ye, brother." She grinned slyly.

He ignored her remark and tried not to think on how right his sister was. "It will no' be yer concern soon enough. Not when Gillean arrives."

"Aye, that bothers me too."

"Surely 'tis no bad thing she has the security of such a marriage? If her father is dead, she has little now."

"Do ye no' see the hurt in her eyes?"

He let his shoulders drop. "Aye, I do."

"A man like Gillean can do her no good. I know what causes that hurt, Finn. I know all too well," she said softly.

"What say ye, sister? Ye speak in riddles."

"I willnae speak on this more than necessary, 'tis in the past and I know how ye shall react..."

This caused Finn to pause and grip her arm. "What do ye speak of, Lorna? Tell me now."

She licked her lips. "Ye know my marriage was no' a happy one."

"I know he was not the most exciting of men. I regret ye were forced into such an alliance but I was assured he could keep ye safe."

"Safe from many things, but no' safe from him," she said bitterly.

"What say ye? He hurt ye?" He grabbed her other arm and held both tightly. "Lorna, ye will tell me the truth."

Lorna lowered her gaze. "Aye. He wasnae a good man."

Finn dropped her arm, stung by her words. Why had he not seen his sister's misery? He snorted inwardly. Because he was too taken up with the battles at Glencolum. Ach, and too taken up in his own grief. For all his fears of having a woman dependant on him, he had failed the one woman who should have been able to turn to him.

"Why did ye no' say?" he asked gruffly.

"'Twas nae yer fight, Finn. 'Tis no matter now, anyhow. He is long dead and I willnae be placed in such a position again."

"Lorna…" He scraped a hand through his hair. "If ye should ever need…"

She rested a hand on his arm. "Ye are a good man, brother. Ye have never failed me. Are ye not here now? Ye put yer life at risk for Katelyn and my husband's family. I willnae

forget that and neither shall Katelyn. We owe ye a great debt."

"Ye owe me naught. But it seems I owe ye much more. Lorna, ye shouldnae have had to suffer…"

Ach, his voice cracked. His sister had needed him and he'd been too blind to see it. Or too stubborn. His reluctance to get close to a woman—even his own kin—had cost Lorna dearly. He would not allow that to happen again.

"Do not think on it anymore."

"If ye had told me…"

"Ye would have what? Killed him."

"Aye," he replied through gritted teeth. "Gladly."

"And ye would have been hanged for yer troubles. I willnae tell ye again, brother. Dinnae think on it. The past is the past."

He eyed his sister and her resolute expression. Fire still kindled under his skin, merging with that sense of powerlessness. The same as when Alice had died. When birthing their babe took her from him, he'd thrown himself into a drunken stupor. Had the child survived, mayhap he would have behaved differently. As it was, he was ashamed of the way he had dealt with his grief. No doubt, Lorna knew well of it, even if they saw little of each other at the time. But his stubborn sister would not have wished to burden him.

Finn sucked in a long breath and affected a calm expression—even managing to smile. All who knew him recognised his ready smile. None understood the turmoil that lay underneath. Apart from, perhaps, his sister.

"As ye bid, little sister."

She arched a knowing brow but did not comment on his patronising tone. Rarely did she not rise to his challenges. Even in their childhood she had been determined to prove herself stronger, faster, and cleverer than he and their cousins. Some days he suspected she was indeed the boldest warrior he knew.

Lorna broke the silence with a quick smile. "And so to Lady Katelyn."

"Aye?"

"If ye are to stay, ye dinnae toy with her, Finn."

Finn tried to look affronted but failed. His sister was far too canny. "I dinnae know what ye mean."

"She needs time and comforting. But she doesnae need ye charming her into bed."

"Come now, I am in no habit of seducing maidens—betrothed maidens at that."

"That I know, but she is a bonny lass, and I am no fool." Lorna propped her hands on her hips. "Ye may act the rogue but ye are honourable and can treat a lass well when ye are doing more than taking a tumble with her. Dinnae take a tumble with her, Finn, ye hear me. Be the gentleman I know ye can be."

Ach, how he wished his sister would not speak of *tumbling* at the same time as speaking of Katelyn. It made his body ache with need. Creamy flesh, glinting emerald eyes, a gently curving smile as he laid his lips to her soft thighs....

"I willnae touch her," he said more sharply than intended.

Lorna rolled her eyes. "See that ye do not."

A retort sat on his tongue but he held it, his sister's admission of Walter's treatment of her fresh in his mind. He do his best not to disappoint her.

"Make yer plans to stay known to Logan. He likes to know all that is going on in the keep."

"Aye, now there's a man who could do with being married off." He laughed as his sister's eyes narrowed. "Yer man, Logan, needs a woman. He doesnae know how to take pleasure in anything."

"Whereas ye take too much," Lorna shot back.

Finn chuckled again. Lorna had a weak spot when it came to Logan. But then Logan had been there when he had not. It appeared he likely owed that man a great debt too. He shook his head, spun away and strode out of the hall in search of Logan.

He caught sight of Katelyn at Logan's side, hair streaming behind her as they strolled across the bailey. He paused and studied the blue skies and purple and orange hills. Inhaling the slightly smoky air, he knew he should not touch her again, for he would surely crumble and give into temptation. However he hoped she would at least visit his bed in his dreams again.

***

Warily, Catriona descended the steps into the Great Hall. The smell of baked bread and roasted meats clung to the air. In front of her, two large tables lined the hall and already the household had gathered for supper. The scrape of eating knives made her wince.

Her chest squeezed and her breaths grew rapid as she tried to block out the images that assailed her. She clenched her eyes shut and steadied herself against the wall. Catriona dragged her heavy lids open, sucked in a deep breath—willed the memories to fade. Descending the last few steps, she found herself confronted by a wide chest in a linen shirt and red plaid. She focused on that torso for a moment, taking in the lines of strength and the sinuous length of his arms. Gradually the world returned and the squashing sensation in her chest dissipated.

She dragged her gaze up, bracing herself for the soft understanding but there was none. His bold stare made her toes curl and her skin heat. She offered him a small smile in return, relieved not to have to suffer yet another look of sympathy. While the maids and Lorna had been kind in their care of her the past few days, the carefulness with which they treated her vexed. Here she was lying to them and they offered nothing but kindness. And the closed walls of the castle and the busy household seemed to compound the experiences of the previous sennight. It was as if the stone held in her fears until they surrounded and suffocated her. Catriona had tried her hardest to rest before supper but, alas, the sights and sounds of battle and death would not leave her.

However, this tall fair haired warrior regarded her as a

woman rather than a wounded creature, coming to seek sanctuary to lick her wounds. And while she was used to men looking at her like that, never had there been such audacity behind the expression. Men usually revered her. Made her into something she was not. As soon as it became apparent she would be a great beauty, she struggled to live up to the impression she gave men. When they flirted, she blushed and cowered away. When she walked into a room and they stared, she lowered her head. And women were no better. Most loathed her on sight because of her looks. Even her sister hated that they shared the same face.

For the first time in her life, she preferred to be looked at with... *lust,* mayhap? Rather than pity. Under Finn's gaze, she forgot she'd been expelled from her home and had come very close to a violent death. In his company, she almost felt deserving of such a look.

If only she was. If only she had the freedom to act upon it.

"Did ye rest well, Katie?"

The low tone to his voice did something strange to her insides. How she wished he knew her real name, her real identity. To hear her name on his lips would surely be worth much risk.

"Aye, well enough," she replied huskily.

"Allow me to take ye to supper." He offered a hand and stepped to the side of her.

Catriona glanced up at him and laid her hand carefully over the top of his. She'd touched him often enough to remember how his skin felt—rough, warm—but it still made her jolt. Skirts held in her other hand, she allowed him to escort her to the top table. Lorna lifted a drink and smiled as Catriona followed Finn around the trestle table to a large chair. Pulling it out, Finn motioned for her to be seated.

Her breath trapped in her chest as she lowered herself. This was the first time she'd eaten in the hall. For the past three days, she'd remained in her room—hiding, mayhap, under the pretence of being shaken. And she was. But also she feared giving herself away. Twice now she had forgotten to respond when someone called her Katelyn.

She concentrated on inhaling slowly. Was it Finn's gaze upon her that did that or the way the servants and men turned to watch her? Did they pity her? Did they know of her experiences at the hands of the Norse? And how it now plagued her mind more and more with every passing moment?

She clutched the oak table and drew her spine straight. With a gentle smile, she dipped her fingers into the bowl a servant offered her and dried her hands on a linen sheet. She needed to remember the role she was to play. Many a noblewoman saw bloodshed and yet they did not crumble like she. But years of being pushed aside and ignored meant she had been most at home in the company of the servants, all of whom had become dear to her. She felt very little like a woman of noble blood.

Finn seated himself next to her, elbow brushing her arm as he did so. He leaned in to murmur an apology and the side of her face heated when his breath breezed over her cheek.

Flustered, and fighting the longing twist of her heart—the one that said she wished he would whisper more words in her ears—she pulled her trencher close and pushed a loose strand of hair behind her still tingling ear.

"How are ye, Katelyn?" Lorna asked between sips of ale. "Have ye rested some?"

"Aye, I thank ye. My chambers are beautifully appointed."

Lorna's lips curved. "It pleases me ye like them. I had a hand in most of the furnishings in the keep. Alas my husband had no eye for these things and even less liking for sparing coin for such frivolities."

"Ye surely have a lovely home," Catriona offered softly. She'd heard enough whispers of what Lorna's marriage had been like—cold, painful, miserable. She understood Lorna's need to surround herself with beautiful things. Once again, she envied the woman her strength.

Lorna cast a look around, her smile slightly wan and Catriona wondered if her thoughts followed her own.

"I must thank ye for all ye have done." Catriona spilled out hastily, wary of causing her hostess distress. "Without ye,

I'd-I'd..." Her voice cracked and she dabbed the linen to her mouth.

A hand pressed to Catriona's arm, Lorna's smile warmed. "Dinnae even think on it. While my men may have been under orders from yer betrothed, I was grateful to be able to help ye. No woman should suffer because of the folly of men. And as we well know, most wars are pure folly."

Catriona pressed her lips together and swallowed. Deceiving such a woman—even for a cause as great as the safety of Bute—seemed so very wrong. How would Lorna feel if the truth was revealed?

"Ye and Finn risked much for me. I am most grateful. In truth, I dinnae know how I shall repay such kindness." She chanced a sideways glance at Finn and noted he was speaking with the man at his side, thank the Lord. He'd seen her at her worst. She did not wish him to witness anymore of her fragility. Snatching her goblet, she took a gulp of ale.

"Ye need not repay it. Yer company is enough. I shall enjoy yer time here until we hear word from Laird Gillean"

Finn coughed, drawing their attention and Catriona twisted to view him. "Aye, I suppose ye ladies shall be busy preparing for the wedding."

"I... I suppose so." Aye, a wedding that should not be hers. "I confess I am ill prepared for it. With the fighting, the marriage arrangements became of little importance."

"I can understand that," Finn agreed. "What gown the bride should wear is hardly something a father should be thinking on at a time of war."

Catriona scowled at his odd tone. "There is more to marriage than a gown," she insisted quietly and Lorna gave her a look of respect.

Finn's brows shot up and he took a long drink before responding, "Well, ye will find that out soon enough, I suppose."

Frustrated by his sulky tone, Catriona turned her attention to her meal. Why did the subject of her marriage rile the man? She jabbed the meat with her eating knife, appetite gone. If only she knew more of Laird Gillean. Katelyn had been told very little of the man and shared even less with her—only boasting on occasion of his wealth. The contract had been signed and sent by messenger over two months ago but none expected Katelyn to become ill or for the island to come under siege. Catriona certainly never anticipated taking Katelyn's place as Laird Gillean's bride. She might have listened more carefully otherwise.

Suddenly the hall seemed too crowded, too noisy. Everyone was watching her and waiting for her to slip up. Looking for cracks in her disguise. Catriona clenched the knife in her hand and saw the tremble of her fingers. The steel tip of the blade turned red before her eyes and the room spun.

Dropping the blade as the scent of blood invaded her imagination, she thrust back her chair and hurried out of the hall.

***

Finn threw down his knife and shared a look with Lorna. Damnation. Had it been what he'd said? He'd been behaving like a boar. The mere mention of her marriage to a man she barely knew set him on edge.

Lorna went to follow after her but Finn put his hand on hers and shook his head. "I shall go to her. 'Twas my fault and ye are still yet a stranger to her."

Lorna nodded. "As ye will."

Scraping a hand through his hair, he stomped across the hall and pushed through the half open door. He took a moment to glance around and spotted her on top of the ramparts, black hair fluttering lightly in the breeze, her pale blue gown billowing behind her. With her arms wrapped around her waist she looked small and vulnerable. The need to add his strength to hers created an ache in his chest.

He would have to apologise though he did not relish such a duty. Still, he had not meant to hurt her. Since their arrival at Kilcree she had become strained and quiet. Her words came out at no more than a whisper, if at all. What had happened to the determined woman he'd met on Bute? Finn shook his head.

And he had added to her worries, whatever those were, with his uncouth words.

He pressed his lips together and studied her, considering what he would say. In truth, he did not know, but he longed to heal her hurts. He shook his head at himself. What was he thinking?

Regardless, he walked up the inner steps, all impatience and heavy legs. Torn between fleeing the hold she had over him and simply clamping her to him and taking her then and there.

Either she was lost in thought or she did not hear him approach as she remained looking out at the hills on the horizon. He paused to observe the slight tilt of her upper lip, the smoothness of her cheeks. This was dangerous. Already he felt more than he should for such a woman.

"Katie?"

She spun and released a tiny sound of surprise. "F-forgive me, I didnae mean to—"

Tears shimmered in her gaze and Finn cut her off by dragging her to him. One hand to the base of her spine, the other on her neck, he trapped her against his chest. She did not crumble as he thought she might. He recognised this woman. The one who insisted on walking barefoot across the Highlands. The one who declared she would keep watch. Her rigid spine and the hold on her emotions assured him that the lass he'd first met was not completely gone.

But eventually she softened into him, like liquid forming to the shape of a bottle. She fit him perfectly. Warm breaths teased his skin at the open collar of his shirt, round breasts crushed against him, and the soft, soft flesh of her neck sent heat curling through him. Desire gathered between his thighs, making him hard.

Could she feel his arousal? Ach, of course she could. Would she think him a blackguard? She made no moves to draw away so he concluded it did not bother her… or mayhap she even welcomed his need for her.

While he prayed the latter, it could not be. Finn mac Chaluim did not bed maidens or betrothed women. He took his pleasure with widows or willing maids. With lasses who wanted a night of shared desire and nothing more.

She belongs to another man, he reminded himself while he inhaled the scent of lavender that clung to her hair.

Or at least she would soon. And he would not ruin her or hurt her further. A man like himself was destined to be alone and that was how he liked it. He did not want to be worrying for Katelyn. He'd done enough of that for Alice and look where that had led him. The deep throb of pain panged in his stomach. He failed to protect her from death and had their baby daughter survived, he probably would have spent the rest of his days worrying for her too. That kind of anxiety, a man could do without.

And he could do without Katelyn.

A shame his body didn't agree. He almost groaned aloud when she finally flung her arms around his waist, pressing herself closer.

"Forgive me, wee lass," he said gruffly. "I didnae mean to be rude."

"Nay," she said, her voice muffled against his chest, "wasnae ye."

He forced out a breath through gritted teeth. For some reason the thought of her marriage to a stranger had twisted something inside him. Would he feel more assured if she knew more of Gillean? If she appeared prepared to devote herself to the man with whom she was to spend the rest of her days?

Mayhap, but he doubted it. In all likelihood, nerves about her coming nuptials were making her quiet. Would that he could soothe such worries, but what could he say? Finn knew little of love or arranged marriages. Not being heir to any great fortune, he had few obligations. Alice was a good woman, from a strong family and he liked her immediately. Theirs was no great love story, but he imagined they could have enjoyed a fine life together had she survived the birth of their child.

The desire to fling her back and storm away struck once more but how could he? Here was a woman who had been caught in a battle waged by men and now she was to be at the mercy of a man once more. He'd never considered how such matters affected women before, but Lorna's pain made him all the more aware of what Katelyn could be walking into. She deserved so much more than that.

"Will ye… will ye tell me what plagues ye, lass?"

She shook her head, face still buried against him. "'Tis no matter."

He clenched his teeth again as that sense of powerlessness threatened to drown him. How to comfort the lass? His experience with women was limited to bedding and flirtations. The only woman he ever truly spoke with was Lorna and, with the clan war, he'd barely seen her of late.

She finally retreated, rubbed the end of her nose and offered him a weak smile. He returned it with a tilted one of his own.

"All is well," she assured.

Ach, as if Katelyn was the one trying to comfort him. He was the warrior, the man. The one who should be looking after her, not the other way around.

Her lips curved upwards as she viewed him. "Truly. Ye dinnae need to regard me so."

He scowled. "How do I regard ye?"

Katelyn tilted her head. "I know not. Yer brow furrows," she reached up and skimmed a finger across his forehead, leaving a blaze of fire in its wake, "as if ye are trying to solve some great riddle."

Letting his scowl drop, he snatched those fingers, making her gasp—toying with fire. And he knew it well. Yet he could not stop. "Ye are a riddle, Katie. I thought I had the measure of ye on our journey but it seems I dinnae."

"I am no riddle." Colour sat high in her cheeks. Her gaze dropped before meeting his boldly once more.

"And yet one moment ye are bold and the next ye are as coy as a young maiden."

She let slip a startled giggle. "I dinnae think I have ever been accused of being coy before."

A grin cracked his face. "It pleases me to see ye smile, lass." His words surprised even him. He hadn't meant to tell her that, but it appeared he lost control of his mouth with Katelyn around. Mayhap it was his need to understand her that drove him or perhaps the desire eating at his gut—a great gnawing ache—made him forget that he did not converse with women.

"Why?"

He blinked.

"Why does it please ye to see me smile?"

"Ye have smiled little these past days and said even less."

Katelyn clasped her hands in front of her and glanced down. "Mayhap I am just a quiet lass."

Finn arched a brow. "Ye cannae fool me. We spoke much

on our journey here, remember?"

"Ye mean *I* did." That teasing smile arrived on her lips again drawing his attention to the lush pink succulence.

"Aye." It was true. He had grown used to her incessant questions and gentle observations. She'd quizzed him on everything—from the surrounding countryside to more personal questions. He told her of Morgann and Alana, and all his kin. He did not allow her to dig any deeper, however. How could he bear the pity in her gaze as he spoke of Alice when he deserved none? Still, she surely knew more of him than any other woman he'd bedded.

Ach, back to bedding! He curled his fist and his groin tightened yet again. Was he to live in a constant state of arousal around Katelyn?

She turned to peer out over the castle wall, hands pressed to the stone. And clearly unaware of his inner turmoil. Katelyn sighed. "I confess, I dinnae enjoy being closeted away much. With the siege, I spent much time hiding behind castle walls… I…" Her voice cracked.

Finn had no choice but to jump to her rescue. He would not see her distressed. "Ye prefer to be on the other side of the wall?"

With a small smile, she nodded, gaze still attached to the horizon. "Aye. Bute is beautiful when not at war. I would give much to be there again, out on the hills or looking over the sea."

"I am sorry." He laid a hand over hers as it rested on the stone.

"Dinnae be. Ye rescued me remember?"

"Would that I could return ye. I would gladly take ye to the hills or to the sea."

"I should like that. It seems I am more at ease with sleeping in the wild than in a fine bed. Alas, I dinnae make a fine noble woman."

Sleeping in the wild? Her words reminded him of a soft body beneath fur. Of it tucked against him. He traced the curve of her breast with his gaze, breaths thickening.

"Ye make a fine noble woman, Katie," he said roughly. *Too fine.*

He swallowed as she drew her hand from underneath his and turned to face him. Her eyes widened. Did she see the need flaring in him? He felt it. Like flaming logs, lust burned bright inside. The thud of his heart grew sickening while she stared on. He saw her throat work, the flutter of her pulse. Her breasts pressed against her bodice, straining the front laces and he flexed his fingers as he imagined them upon those laces, drawing them out.

Behind him, the chatter of men and footsteps sounded, snapping his attention away. Finn let his shoulders drop. Relieved? Mayhap. Disappointed? Likely. He shook his head at himself and watched as the men left the hall and returned to their stations.

"I shall take my leave," he said brusquely, dropping his head briefly. When he raised his gaze, he saw Katelyn's startled expression and realised he'd been too abrupt. But he had to escape. The draw of this woman was too powerful. Already he cared too much for her welfare. Before long he'd be spending his days and nights worrying for her and what then?

Nothing. For she would be in another man's arms soon. Even if she was not to be wed, he could not care for such a lass. Better to stay alone than risk pain again.

Hastily, he descended the inner steps and pushed his way past another man, mumbling an apology as he made for the hall. He had need of ale. And quickly.

***

From her view point at the very top of the castle, Tèile let her wings drop. That had been close. Yet again. Mayhap those dreams weren't such a good idea. She hadn't gifted Finn with any since he met Katelyn but it seemed he still dreamed of her. Now she was fighting a battle against their desire. And in spite of Catriona's reservations, it was clear the woman wanted Finn just as badly.

But desire was not enough. This needed to be a love match. If they indulged too quickly and at the wrong time,

Tèile's carefully crafted plans would fall apart. If she was to get fate back on the right path, she'd have to watch over these two very closely. What should have been a slow and natural courtship now blazed with need and anxiety. Catriona's disguise did not help, nor did the impending arrival of Laird Gillean. Catriona should have met Finn on Bute as herself when he came for Katelyn, but alas, her storms had convinced the Norsemen to bring forward their invasion campaign. Curses.

Of course, she could delay the laird, but that would mean more magic and more trickery. How she hated having her hands tied, but she had learned the hard way not to meddle any more than necessary. Should she throw things out of balance yet again, she may never return to the fae world. Tèile kicked a tiny pebble from the ramparts and huffed.

This human world was too harsh, too cold for a green faery like her. All grey stone and swords and fighting. She longed to be feasting with her friends and enjoying nature. Tèile smoothed a hand across the stone and admitted to herself that there was some warmth in the human world. Alana and Morgann had taught her that. But would Finn and Catriona do the same?

***

Smoke from the candles and the smell of crisp, clean hay welcomed Finn as he entered the stables. He inhaled deeply and made his way over to his mount. She whinnied in greeting. He put a hand to her muzzle and grinned.

"At least ye dinnae cause me any problems, Dìleas. Ye are one lass I dinnae need to worry for."

His mind hazy from ale, he rubbed down her flanks as she pushed against him. It should have soothed him. Time with his faithful horse usually did. She'd seen him through battles and long journeys, and had never faltered, never become ill or weak. If he could only find a woman like that.

Finn scowled. Katelyn had never faltered on their journey. But he didn't want Katelyn. Something had her upset and it beleaguered him. If he worried over her when he barely knew her, what would happen if he let her work any deeper into his thoughts?

He clenched his fist. Not that he would.

Giving Dìleas one last pat, he strolled to the end of the stables and leaned against the wooden frame. Torches flickered in their mounts and the distant hoot of an owl punctuated the quiet shuffle of men patrolling the walls. High up in the keep a golden glow emanated from Katelyn's chamber. The shutters were still open. Did she look out and think of him? Did raw, painful need heat her body too? All he had to do was think of her—her upturned lips, pearly skin and raven hair—and he grew hard.

Finn slapped a palm against the wood. This would not do. He'd been content with life before Katelyn. He had his kinsmen and his duties, his simple cottage at Glencolum and the company of the occasional maid in his bed. He wanted for nothing and that was how he liked it.

Teeth clenched, he turned away from the taunting light of her window and stepped into the nearest stall. He adjusted his arousal with a hiss and slumped onto a hay bale. Leaning his head against the wood, he pressed a breath out and closed his eyes. His lip tingled at the memory of her fingers skimming over it. What he would not give to feel those fingers on his other scars. She would touch him boldly, he decided, while looking at him with a coy expression on her face. With her lip tucked between her teeth, green eyes glistening with curiosity and desire, those gentle fingers would trace his body.

The ache between his thighs became too much and he wrapped a hand around his manhood, nearly groaning aloud at the pleasure suffused with pain. His rough palm was no match for how Katelyn's fingers likely felt but he had little other choice. With strong movements, he recalled the flash of a thigh or a breast as he enclosed her in that fur. He imagined parting those thighs and losing himself to her.

For he surely would lose himself in her sweet heat as she called his name and begged for more. Powerless as he was, he would give her his all and her explosive response might be the end for him.

Sweat pricked his forehead when he worked harder, the sensations building. Ach, how he needed the taste of her lips, to hear her ragged breaths mingling with his own. Finn gripped the straw while his climax built. In his mind, he was lost in Katelyn's body, spilling himself in her and claiming her as his and not some other man's.

"Not another man's," he growled to himself as he jerked and his release swallowed him.

Gathering his breath, he lifted his head and opened his eyes before slumping back again. He did not feel nearly satisfied enough. The twist in his gut told him he'd only find satisfaction with one woman and she was to be another's. And there was little to be done about it.

CHAPTER FIVE

Catriona took a turn around the keep, pausing to admire a scattering of wildflowers. She crouched and picked a few blooms. Supressing a yawn, she admired the tiny yellow flower. Fatigue made her head ache and her mouth dry. Sleep did not come easily since coming to the castle. Dreams of blood and violence, of rough hands, haunted her. Occasionally they were broken by visions of a fair haired warrior but that left her aching and wanting. Who knew which dream was better?

"Pretty," she murmured as she pressed the bloom against her lips.

"Pretty indeed," a deep male voice came.

Catriona's heart stuttered when she turned her head to come face to face with leather boots and great sturdy legs. Her gaze followed them up and up until she reached Finn's face.

The large man smiled down at her, making her stomach do a tiny dance. Hastening to her feet, she swiped her hands down her skirts and dipped her head.

"Good morrow."

Her gown squeezed the air from her. And it was not like when her terrors consumed her. Normally that left her chilled. Nay, as she studied him, his wide shoulders and his confident stance, her skin grew hot and clammy. He stared at her and she stared back but for the life of her she couldn't look away. Those blue eyes scorched her very soul.

"May I?" He opened a hand.

Startled, it took her an instant to decipher what he wanted. She dropped the flower into his palm, marvelling at the sight of something so delicate against those large, blunt hands. His fingers brushed her hair aside first, sending a tremor of anticipation through her. His warm gaze lingered on her, trapping her. She willed her limbs to move, to shy away from him, but they remained stiff. Rough fingers slid the stem of the bloom behind her ear. He took a moment to adjust it. Catriona found herself aware of every slight touch and it made her tremble. Her breaths were loud and rasping in her ears.

"There," he announced and stepped back. "Very pretty."

"Thank ye," she whispered.

She shook her head, heat burning at her cheeks under his intense look. No man had ever looked at her quite like that.

While the looks she garnered normally ran from uncertainty to salaciousness, his bordered on... on indecent. And it made her body clench in an utterly unfamiliar way. She recalled the solid length of his arousal flattened against her and the way it made her feel. Two days had passed since then yet it excited her even now.

He broke the connection as Logan called his name from behind. He dipped his head and gave her a slanted grin. "If ye'll excuse me, Katie. 'Tis time for weapons practice and I must show these men how 'tis done."

His self-assurance made her chuckle. "As ye will. I shall pray yer confidence is not misplaced."

"Ach, ye have seen me in action, lass, do ye doubt me?"

"Nay," she admitted, "I dinnae doubt ye. Fight well, Finn, and dinnae be harmed."

"Ye have my word, my lady." With another dip, he left her but not before offering her a wink that made heat climb her chest.

Shaking her head at the confusing man, Catriona continued her stroll around the castle. The day was dry and sunny but it had rained overnight, leaving the ground muddy underfoot.

She followed the wall around the keep, tracing along the rough stone. Still no word from her father. How much longer would she have to wait? Many more days and Laird Gillean would have her as his wife. She shuddered. While she knew little of him, greed clearly drove him. A man who threatened war to gain a bride and wealth could not be a good one. While Katelyn might have been content to be used so, she could not bring herself to be. Mayhap Katelyn would have been happy in such a marriage, had her father even planned to go through with it. It was a stalling tactic, nothing more. As soon as he gained support from the king, the marriage contract would mean nothing. But still, Katelyn might have found happiness with someone as greedy and as driven as she.

Catriona had only ever wanted a man who cared for her. Not her wealth or her family name. Nor for her looks. But no man had ever revealed himself to be anything but driven by hunger. For beauty or wealth.

Aside from perhaps Finn. As much as she wanted to ignore it, she had a need of her own for that man. He proved vastly different to anyone she had ever encountered. Aye, he looked at her as if he might pounce upon her and bring her wild pleasure beyond her imaginings but he also treated her with respect, as if he valued her words and ideas.

Another yawn fought its way out and dread made her stomach cramp. She began to fear the evenings when she would be trapped in her chambers with only her thoughts. Why could she not focus on anything but the horrors of the siege? She fisted a hand. Her mother had taught her to make the best of each situation. Where was her dignity when the dreams made her fling herself about her room? Or when the thoughts became too much and crowded her mind, forcing her to run away?

She paused as a sound sent a shiver through her. The clanging of swords. Catriona was back in the cold passageway, pressed against the sharp stone, her heart beating in her ears as the Viking approached. She continued around the castle toward the sound and shook away the memory. Shoulders straight, she drew her chin up. She *would* conquer her fears.

The noise came from Finn and another man, duelling with swords. The use of real blades made her frown. Her hand went to her mouth when the blade of his opponent swiped so very close to Finn's arm. So dangerous.

But she was also fascinated. He moved well—gracefully. She'd witnessed him fighting before but had been too consumed by fear to truly watch. A lot of men's movements were usually powered by aggression but with Finn it was different. Each move appeared carefully considered and planned. Emotion did not rule his actions. She sighed. If only she could be the same.

He took down his opponent easily and the man offered up his palms in surrender with a grin. Another man stepped forward and so began another fight. Finn battled harder this time as his dark haired enemy was large. It did not surprise

Katelyn when he forced the man's sword out of his hand and urged him to his knees with a quick grin.

When Finn brought his blade to the man's neck, it happened. Her throat grew tight and clogged. Dots danced in front of her vision. She meant to turn away but her head swam and she tried to suck in breaths while scrabbling for a hold on something. Heart beating rapidly, she pressed a hand to her chest and rubbed at it in a bid to draw in some air but it was useless. Darkness crowded her mind and the world tilted away.

Footsteps and voices echoed in her ears and something pressed underneath her. She struggled to open her eyes and draw breath but panic still gripped her, forcing her to curl up. And then she was floating, cradled by two strong arms. It should have made the sensations worse but somehow the warmth of those arms eased the constriction in her throat and she sucked in several ragged breaths.

Still weak and fighting the images in her mind, Catriona kept her eyes shut. She vaguely heard Lorna's voice and then footsteps on wood. They were carrying her to her chambers, she realised. Soft blankets swallowed her as she was laid down, their herby fragrance comforting. She longed to stay locked in the dark abyss. Safe from life and the demons that shadowed her every step.

***

Finn jerked awake, heart pounding unnaturally. He scowled, lay there for a moment and stared at the fabric canopy above him. He strained to listen. What had woken him? He rubbed his arm. It tingled and he was sure something had jabbed him.

An odd sound stopped his eyelids from falling closed again and he sat. Was that crying? Screaming? It was faint but it certainly sounded like a woman. Climbing from the bed, he grabbed the shirt he'd flung carelessly over the chair in the corner and left the laces loose. Night still reigned and only splinters of silvered moonlight seeped in through the shutters to guide his way.

Nearly stubbing his toe on the end of the bed, he hastened to the door and tossed it open. The torches were still lit and the one outside his chamber stuttered with the sudden gust. He paused in the doorway. Aye, a woman to be sure. And the tightness in his chest told him he knew which woman it was.

Katelyn.

He strode along the corridor that linked the chambers. The sound increased and even though he told himself she couldn't be in danger, the tension in his gut amplified.

Ready for anything, he eased open Katelyn's door. It squeaked on its hinges and he grimaced. But no one attacked him. Indeed, the only person in the room was Katelyn. Lying on her side, the torchlight from the corridor revealed the long length of her thigh and her magnificent hair cascading down her back, clearly having come free from a braid. His racing heart slowed as he studied her. The blankets were entirely gone, kicked off onto the floor. She hadn't bothered drawing the curtains around the bed. The weather had not been cold enough for that.

So Finn had a glorious view of that incredible figure encased in a whisper of a chemise.

Before his body responded to the sight, she tossed suddenly, a whimper coming from her lips. Finn stiffened as her anguished expression became apparent. She did it again, moving quickly and frantically, and her whimpers turned to cries. He watched, took a step forward and paused. Should he wake her? Would she be embarrassed to find him in her chamber?

She made the decision for him when she nearly flung herself off the bed. If he didn't act, she would surely harm herself. Quickly coming to her side, he caught her when she rolled again and urged her gently onto the bed with him. Sweat clung to her brow and it dampened his shirt as he bundled her into his arms and pressed her hard against him. Katelyn fought him but the noises quietened to a soft sob. The sound pierced him, like a knife wound. He'd seen this before, especially in men who had witnessed battle for the first time but he didn't know women could suffer the same.

When she ceased fighting him, her breathing slowed but still she cried. He stroked her cheek, felt dampness there and softly urged her to awaken. Katelyn tensed abruptly and he knew she was finally awake. But she couldn't stop crying.

Ach, powerless yet again.

Finn raised her face to his. The golden glow of the torches still crept in through the open door so he saw the pain in her eyes. Katelyn didn't look away or bury herself against his chest as he thought she might do. It appeared as though she was incapable. She sobbed openly, uncontrollably and he had to watch every heart-breaking moment of it.

Unable to bear her pain any longer and refusing to question why that hurt anguished him so much, he did the only thing he could think of to soothe away her tears.

He kissed her.

She tasted salty and wet at first. And she still wept but the sound quietened, giving way to slow, heavy breaths. Katelyn opened her mouth to him while he cradled her head, a hand speared into her hair, the other stroking away the tears on her cheek.

He groaned as the tang of salt was replaced with the flavour of Katelyn. Her tongue tentatively met his and his body instantly inflamed, became tight with need. He hadn't realised she would taste so good. One sample would never be enough now. He pressed deeper and relished her sharp intake of breath. That sweet, supple body grew pliant and aligned with his. Awareness of how big and strong he was seeped in. Something about Katelyn brought out his need to protect.

Removing his hand from her cheek, he trailed his fingers down her side, the heat of her skin almost scalding him. The soft swell of a breast, the indent of her waist, the line of a hip that begged to be grabbed. He needed to claim and defend this vulnerable woman so badly.

But somewhere in the back of his mind, he recalled he'd merely intended to comfort. This was not about him. That didn't mean he could stop though. Not yet. He tilted his head to press the kiss deeper and gave in to the urge to grab her hip. His fingers pressed into the yielding flesh of her rear and he kept her close, the warmth their embrace created sending wild sensations bolting through him. Desire and possessiveness controlled his movements. Having Katelyn in his arms threatened to overcome every belief he'd carefully instilled in himself throughout the years.

A tiny whimper broke the moment. Though she didn't seem ready to end the kiss —the nails digging into his shoulder led him to believe she was enjoying it as much as he—the reason he'd kissed her came flooding back. Gently, carefully, he slowed the kiss, touching her tongue once more and silently wishing he could repeat the experience. Then he broke away but kept her in his hold. Katelyn accepted his comfort easily and burrowed against his chest. Her arms snaked around his waist and his heart swelled at the trust this lass put in him. She barely knew him yet she was willingly sharing her grief with him. It seemed the exquisite Katelyn was stronger than she appeared.

After many torturous moments of having her flattened against him, he spoke. "Are ye well, lass?"

She nodded against his torso.

"Ye suffer with dreams," he stated gently.

"Aye," she whispered.

"What do ye see? Can ye tell me?"

He heard her gulp and her body stiffened so he stroked up and down her back until she relaxed again.

"Blood..." Her voice was so quiet he had to strain to hear her. "So much blood. The Viking..."

"Ye mean when ye were attacked..."

"Aye."

"How long have ye been having these dreams?"

"Ever since we arrived at Kilcree," she replied quietly. "'Twas why I swooned yesterday."

He nodded. That explained much. Her sudden fragility, her strange moods and that fainting fit. It relieved him that it was at least not some illness. She had spent the rest of the day abed and insisted she needed no healer.

"I am consumed by demons." Her voice hitched.

"Nay." He tugged her back and forced her face up to his with a finger under her chin. "Nay, not by demons. Dinnae ever say such a thing again. I have seen grown men, bigger and stronger than I, taken by the same thing. They cry and whimper like bairns. Ye are stronger even than them, Katie. Any fool can see that. How many would admit to such fears and dreams? None, I'd wager."

She dropped her gaze but he kept the finger under her chin, forcing her to look at him again. His words were seeping in, he was sure, but would they have any effect?

"I am sorry ye saw me like that."

Finn shook his head. "Dinnae be sorry, I am glad."

"Why did ye come?"

"I heard ye."

"Ye could have left me."

"Nay, I couldnae." He secured her with a look and something inside squeezed at the sight of her spiked lashes and shimmering eyes.

Here was a woman so vulnerable and confused, and yet he still desired her more than anything. And if her kiss was anything to go by, she desired him too. But it meant little. While the kiss might have worked to calm her, it was a mistake. She stiffened, as if her thoughts had run the same route. He brushed a kiss across her head and sighed. Katelyn had a long way to go and an uncertain future ahead of her. And *he* would have little to do with it.

She slid out of his hold and arranged her shift around her. She probably didn't realise that the laces on the front were loose and he spied the curve of one perfect breast as she shifted. Hands clasped tightly in front of her, she studied him with wide eyes. Even with the gilded glow of the torches, he saw the heat in her cheeks. Was she imagining similar things to him? Did she wonder how it might feel if their flesh connected? He climbed off the bed and straightened his shirt, aware of his bare legs beneath it.

"Forgive me for waking ye," she murmured, quickly lowering her gaze.

"Dinnae apologise, lass. I'm glad ye did. Ye shouldnae keep these things to yerself. It doesnae do the mind any good, keeping yer fears locked away."

Katelyn raised her head. "Do ye share yers?"

He tensed his jaw and laughed inwardly. Of course he did not. A highlander was not meant to be afraid. Instead of admitting as much, he grinned. "I have no fears, Katie." The disappointment in her expression made him feel a fool so he spoke quickly to erase the look. "Will ye be all right now?"

Her shoulders straightened as she sucked in a deep breath. "Aye, thank ye, Finn."

Finn studied her for a moment and shook his head. "Yer a

daft lass. I think I shall keep ye company this night."

Her eyes widened once more. "What?"

"I can watch over ye while ye sleep if ye like," he explained. Though he had to admit, he could think of better ways to spend the night.

A grateful smile spread across her face, lighting her expression. If only he could make her smile more often.

"Aye, I would like that, thank ye."

Disturbed by her gratitude and the way it made his heart bound, he nodded brusquely. "Get yerself to bed then." He closed the door slowly, focusing on the wood while she picked up the blankets and rearranged them. Once he was sure she was settled, he strode over to the chair in the corner and sat. It took all his restraint not to jump up and offer to watch over her from a much closer distance. "I willnae be here on the morrow, lass," he whispered. "'Twould not do for me to be seen leaving yer chambers."

"Aye," she whispered back. "Good night, Finn."

Ach, like a knife to his heart. He loved hearing his name on her lips. "Good night, Katelyn."

***

A tickle roused Catriona. Something danced over her arm and she swept it away with a grumble. Slowly she peeled open her eyes to see one of the maids, Mae. Catriona sat with a jolt. Sweet Mary, she'd slept through the night. No dreams, no shortness of breath. Normally she woke covered in sweat and struggling to breathe. She considered her body and all seemed fine. Apparently Finn's presence meant she hadn't hurt herself either. Bruises and scratches were becoming a regular thing. She wasn't sure what she did at night but sometimes she awoke on the floor.

"Come on, milady, 'tis late," Mae urged her out of the bed with an arm wrapped around her shoulder. The brown-haired woman paused and eyed her. "Ye look well rested, milady."

Katelyn heard the surprise in Mae's voice and peeked at the chair where Finn had spent the night. She understood Mae's wonder. The maid witnessed her dishevelled state each morning.

"I am well rested, Mae," she replied softly, glancing at the seat once more. There was no sign Finn had been there but she sensed him in the air. For the first time since coming to Kilcree, she had slept. The large warrior soothed away her fears.

Catriona took the chance to study herself and dipped a swatch of linen into the steaming bowl of water Mae had put out for her. Nay, no bruises or scratches. She truly had slumbered well. Warmth rushed into her cheeks when Mae helped her change into an emerald green gown and she recalled the sensation of much stronger fingers spanning her waist. She traced the golden embroidery on the front. Who knew why she returned the kiss or why he even kissed her, but being pressed up against that unforgiving chest, secure in his hold calmed her more than any tonic could. It seemed Finn was the answer to her problems.

Or mayhap not. Finn complicated an already difficult situation. It could be only days until Laird Gillean arrived and claimed her hand. With his plan to marry her—or Katelyn—at Kilcree so she needed no escort to his lands, her disguise could come unravelled before she heard from her father. Or else, she would have to continue the ruse and marry the man. Where would that leave her? Trapped in a marriage to a man who had threatened her father with war. At least until word of Katelyn's death reached him. Then who knew what might happen?

She scowled and raised her arms, allowing Mae to secure a girdle around her hips. Her lips tingled. She'd have to see if they were as swollen as they felt. His kisses were like magic, working where nothing else had.

Catriona rubbed her heated cheeks and sat obediently on the bed to allow Mae to do her hair.

"Yer quiet, milady," Mae commented.

"Aye, forgive me, Mae. I have a lot to think on."

Mae squeezed her arm. "I know, milady. All will be well, I am sure. Yer betrothed will be arriving soon."

Catriona stifled a response about the laird. Her failure to

play the coy bride might draw attention though she imagined Katelyn's behaviour would have been no better. Either she would have revelled in her upcoming wedding to a powerful man or played the spoiled lady and demanded a great celebration. Neither came naturally to Catriona. If she ever married—assuming she escaped her current predicament—she wanted love and a small ceremony. Power did little for her. She'd seen how it corrupted. Once, Katelyn had not been unlike her but as beauty increased and time passed, Katelyn became more like their father. Always wanting more, her every move was carefully considered. With the passing of their mother, Catriona found herself truly alone. Only the servants and villagers could be called her friends.

Despair sat in the pit of her stomach and she drew her shoulders up, refusing to succumb to such thoughts. As much as last night had been a mistake, Finn lent her a sense of strength and she was going to fight these demons and claim back her life on Bute. The thought of her seeing her friends again sent warmth to replace the anguish and she smiled.

***

Stretching her spindly arms, Tèile frowned as she spotted Catriona's smile. She turned and peered out the gap in the shutters and grimaced. Dawn had been and gone and Tèile had slept the entire night. Watching, waiting and following took its toll on her delicate wings and had fatigued her. She suspected the boredom wearied her most of all. A faery really wasn't made for just sitting around and biding her time. However, in a few days' time she could put her plans into action and encourage Finn and Catriona's first kiss. A few dreams and a little accident or two—maybe Catriona could trip into Finn's arms—and fate would be on track. Finn would be so enamoured, he would surely challenge Laird Gillean for her hand.

She peered at the woman again and narrowed her eyes. Tèile recognised that smile. She'd seen it on Alana's face. And that glazed look in her eyes…. The faery curled her hands and shook her head. Something had happened. Her fingertips tingled as if fate had truly slipped from her hands over night.

Something *had* happened. Something had changed.

***

Catriona yelped and the seamstress, Beth, murmured an apology. Resisting the urge to rub her side, she kept her arms raised as Beth fitted the pale blue material to her body.

Lorna nodded approvingly. "Ye suit this shade, Katelyn."

The afternoon sun warmed the solar, enhancing the plush red fabrics of Lorna's chambers. Gold embroidery and pearls reflected the sunlight, and gilded Lorna's fair hair. It struck her how at home the lady appeared in the warm room, surrounded by an intricately carved bed and ornate iron candelabras. Unlike her.

Fingering the silk, Catriona crushed a sigh. This gown meant she was one step closer to marrying Gillean. It sat heavily on her hips, threatened to weigh her down. Or was that the thought of her impending nuptials?

The seamstress came to her feet and stepped back. "'Twill take me a few days to finish the embroidery," she told Lorna.

Indignation heated Catriona's skin. How long would she have to stand around and accept her fate being dictated by others? The laird was funding their wedding and as such, Lorna had taken on all the preparations. With her naturally commanding nature, Lorna thrived on such tasks and had it been anything else, Catriona might have been grateful to her, but not on this—not when it was her future.

"What troubles ye?" Lorna's brow furrowed. "Do ye no' like the colour? Blue is traditional for brides."

"Nay, the colour doesnae trouble me."

Lorna took a step forward and grasped Catriona's hand. "Tell me," she said quietly, "are ye nervous? I know yer mother passed when ye were young. I can offer ye a word or two...."

Now Lorna surely had to see the warmth in her cheeks. "Nay, nay, 'tis nae that. I know well enough what..." She glanced at Beth and Lorna motioned for her to leave. With a curtsey, the woman scurried away and closed the door to the solar. The creaking hinges made Catriona wince.

Lorna urged her to sit on the bed and sat beside her. Catriona ran her fingers over the thick blanket, unable to meet Lorna's gaze. The last thing she needed to be thinking of was the marriage bed, not after how Finn had kissed her. Not now that all she thought on was his powerful arms and strong hands and how enticing they might be against her skin.

"I am aware I'm only a few summers older than ye but should ye need anyone…."

Guilt jabbed her. Lorna had shown her nothing but kindness. Her only sin was being connected by marriage to an ungodly man. Catriona offered her a small smile. "I thank ye, Lorna, for yer care and hospitality. However, I dinnae need any advice. I may not be worldly, but I am no fool either."

Lorna laughed suddenly. "I dinnae think ye a fool at all, Katelyn. Far from it. But ye are clearly no' happy here. Would that I could offer ye some comfort. I know I should have liked some kind words before my own marriage. Indeed the only person I know not to have suffered an arranged marriage was Finn."

"Finn is married?"

"Was."

Catriona managed to stop the sigh of relief releasing. To think she might have been lusting after another's husband! Finn had told her much of his life at Glencolum on their journey. He described the castle, his cottage and lands with such a smile on his face that it made her long to visit. But he had lost a wife. No wonder he never made mention of it.

"What happened?"

"'Twas a long time ago. She, Alice, died giving birth. The babe died with her—a girl."

"I didnae know."

"Finn doesnae speak on it. In truth, I know little myself. I was married off by then and we scarcely saw Finn while a clan war raged on Glencolum lands." Catriona caught the sadness in Lorna's eyes before her expression shuttered.

"I am sorry."

Lorna waved a hand. "Well, my point is that should ye need someone to speak with..."

"Be assured I have no fears about my impending nuptials." Aside from the fact they might actually happen, she corrected herself.

The marriage bed held little interest to her until recently. Until Finn. She'd been around enough animals and lovers to know what it entailed, heard enough gossip to understand the pleasure it might bring—had even become confident in the art of her own pleasure—but never had she considered how it would feel to take a lover. Finn's arousal pressing into her skirts as he held her that day on the wall or when he had kissed her so passionately sparked all kinds of imaginings.

"Will ye no' tell me what plagues ye then, Katelyn?"

Jerking from her thoughts, Catriona looked into Lorna's pale blue eyes—eyes that were so very similar to her brothers—and patted Lorna's hand. *Yer brother*, she wanted to say, even as the words in her mind made her face burn. She hadn't seen him since last night. What did he think of that kiss? Mayhap it had been nothing more than a move to comfort her. Mayhap it meant little to him.

"Naught," she assured Lorna, "save that it has been a trying time and… and I miss my home."

Why did she admit to that? Was it Lorna's kindness or a need to at least share some of her worries?

Lorna nodded slowly. "That I can understand, but ye will Make yerself a new home before long, just as I did here." She motioned around the elegant room. "And a new family too."

With a wry smile, Catriona toyed with the folds of her gown as she considered her dead sister and cruel father. "A new family might be pleasant. I confess there are some people I dinnae miss on Bute."

"Ye have been mistreated," Lorna mused and that slight dip of sorrow creased her brow briefly.

Catriona longed to understand what caused those momentary flashes of pain almost as much as Lorna patently wanted the same from her. In any other circumstances they could be good friends and share whatever ills burdened them, but secrets and a foolish promise still held her back.

Straightening, Catriona squeezed Lorna's hand. "I am well enough. I have suffered no worse than anyone else. Indeed, I have been well-treated most of my life. The siege and all that has happened since has been... a trial, but naught I cannot overcome."

She spoke the truth. Aye, her father was no loving man but she had the servants who had helped raise her show her what true kindness was—and the memories of her mother. Time away from the keep—and her family—had usually kept her in positive spirits. Who could live on such a beautiful island and not be content?

"Ye sound so very much like me," Lorna observed with a grin. She chuckled. "Alas, I know many men, my brother included, who would think us fragile wee things, but they shouldnae underestimate us womenfolk."

Catriona failed to resist a giggle at Lorna's determined tone. The woman was surely a force with which to be reckoned. "I dinnae think anyone would underestimate ye, Lorna. A stronger woman I have never met."

The woman tucked a strand of fair hair behind her ear and tilted her lips. "My men are well used to listening to my commands and will fight long and hard for me, but there are many who are anxious for the day I have a new husband."

"And that day shall be soon?"

"If Laird Gillean has anything to do with it, aye. But I have fought off any potential suitors so far. Mayhap I can continue to seem unmarriageable and I shall spend the rest of my days alone."

"Alone? Surely not? And all yer men seem most loyal. Why, Logan...."

A creak of hinges made her head snap around and Finn ducked into the room, looking sheepish.

"Forgive me...."

Lorna got to her feet and Catriona followed suit, smoothing the heavy silk over her hips. Finn stared at her, his gaze tracing her from head to toe and she dropped her gaze to the floor, hands clenched tightly in front.

"Finn?" Lorna prompted. "What is so urgent that ye must enter my chambers without even a knock?"

"What?"

Catriona lifted her head to see his confused expression. He blinked and snapped his attention to his sister.

"Oh, aye, a rider just arrived. From Laird Gillean. He has been sent ahead of his master who is about two days' ride away. He craves a word with ye."

Catriona squeezed her fingers until her nails dug into the backs of her hands. Two days? And no word from her father yet. The journey from Bute was a sennight at least. She only hoped he had already left and had just had little chance to send a message.

"I see." Lorna smiled quickly, barely disguising the apprehension in her expression. "Well, I shall see ye at supper, Katelyn."

"Aye, good day to ye, Lorna." Catriona fought the need to rub her chest. Why did Lorna appear so apprehensive? Did she know something Catriona did not?

Lorna brushed past Finn, leaving him standing in the doorway. The tightness in her chest increased, but no longer from fear.

"So... this is yer wedding gown?"

"Oh." She brushed her hands over the bodice and glanced at the gown. "Aye... aye it is."

"Ye look very fine in it, Katie."

"Thank ye," she murmured.

Sweet Mary, had the room grown hot? Her bodice was too tight. Her nipples jabbed against the hard fabric as his gaze roved over her. Tingling lips reminded her of his kiss, his heated tongue, his stubble grazing her. The idea that mayhap he thought little of their kiss seemed foolish now he looked at her so intently. He considered her lips, indicating he too was recalling their embrace. But was his attraction to her driven by anything more than a man's need for a woman?

And why did she care?

Nothing could come of this, she reminded herself yet again. Hopefully she'd be gone soon enough. *If* her father ever came for her.

Finn took a sudden step forward and she released a startled sound, retreating so the back of her legs hit the bed. He didn't frighten her—not like the Viking had—but a well of need and frustration in her stomach bubbled up and threatened any remaining composure.

He towered over her, allowing her to study him closely. The tiny scar on his lip taunted her, begged her to dash her tongue over it. Extra golden stubble graced his jaw and she had to clamp her hand to her side to prevent herself from grazing her nails across it. His brows nearly knitted and it occurred to her how odd it was not to see him smile. Even in the most serious of moments, Finn could be counted on to break into a grin. She tried to swallow but her arid throat refused to cooperate.

Dazzling blue eyes bore into her. The back of his hand skimming her cheek startled her and she flinched. He dropped the hand but remained close. The warmth emanating from him sucked the air from the room until she feared she might swoon.

"Did ye rest well?" he finally asked, after an eternity of silence and staring.

"Aye, very well," she rasped. "Thank ye."

"Good." Finn considered her gown and took an abrupt

step back. "Good. Ye'll... ye'll need to be well rested for yer wedding."

The sudden distance and coldness to his tone disconcerted her. Had she been wrong? Had he only been comforting her and now feared she had the wrong idea? "I... I suppose so...."

"Well." He rocked back on his heels and she watched his chest heave as he drew in a breath. "Well, I shall bid ye good day." He spun on one heel and paused, speaking to her over his shoulder. "Ye really do look very fine."

Catriona nodded numbly as he dipped his head and left, drawing the door shut slowly. She sank onto the bed and rubbed her chest. What had that been about? Where had her cheerful, confident Finn gone? The one who offered her such words of solace last night? He had been so *uneasy*. A sudden shard of doubt struck her heart and she rubbed harder at the aching spot. Had he discovered her?

***

Finn stared at the door for a moment. The sound of creaking ropes told him she'd slumped onto the bed. What a fool he must have seemed. Yet, surely she felt the same. The desire shimmering in her gaze practically begged him to throw her on the bed and plunge into her. It had taken all his willpower not to behave a barbarian and take her then and there.

But the gentleman buried deep down saw her confusion and fear. She'd been scared of him. Or mayhap of her need? He couldn't be sure but he never wished to frighten her with his hunger. He spun away and leaned on the cold wall. Slamming a palm against the stone, he lifted his gaze to the wooden rafters and sighed. He needed an ale. That empty ache in his throat had to be quenched by something for it could not be satisfied by Katelyn—a frightened, unsure maiden with a wedding only days away.

He put a hand over his face and shook his head. Why did he forget that whenever he was in her company? The last thing she needed was a broken man who could offer her nothing more than a few hours pleasure. He would be very bad for Katelyn indeed. Likely Laird Gillean would break off the contract should he discover her innocence had been taken.

Not that it would. Finn might not be the most honourable of men, but he would never stoop so low as to ruin a lass's future with one simple act. Not that it would ever be simple between them. And that sent a chill down his spine more than anything. Already, she'd sucked him in too deep. Who knew what would happen if he lost himself to her body for a while?

Dropping his hand from his face, he drew himself up and pushed away from the wall. A few more days and she'd be gone. A few more days of resisting temptation and he could return home. He smirked inwardly. In truth, nothing kept him now but he needed to see this through. He had to hand her over to Gillean and put her from his mind, not to mention he wanted to offer Lorna support while the laird visited. He'd been a neglectful enough brother as it was. A little more time was a small enough sacrifice to make.

Grip tight on the wooden railing, he descended the stairs into the hall. Ah, good, some ale remained from the midday meal. He strode purposefully over to the rear table, squinting as bright sunlight spilled over the white linen. Ale in hand, he poured himself a large cup and drank it down quickly. Ach, he needed something stronger. Mead, mayhap, but it would do. He helped himself to another cup while servants and men-at-arms continued with their duties. The slight warmth loosened his muscles and he debated the bottom of the earthenware beaker for a moment.

A hand to his shoulder drew him from his thoughts and he spun to see Logan staring him down with a raised eyebrow. "Ye'll no' find any answers in the bottom of that."

Finn contemplated the cup again and released a sharp breath before dropping it to the table. "Yer right."

"What troubles ye, my friend?"

"Naught more than usual."

"So our guest doesnae bother ye?"

"Bother me?" He feigned confusion. "Why should she

bother me?"

Logan laughed and shook his head. "Dinnae take me for a fool, Finn. Yer sister may not be able to see it, but I know a man on the verge of love when I see one."

"Love? Logan, have ye been indulging in the devil's brew?" What on God's earth made Logan think such a thing. Love? Ach, just the word turned his stomach.

"My role as protector of the keep affords me much time to watch and learn. And I know enough of love."

Finn narrowed his eyes. As far as he knew, Logan had never been in love or even close. The man rarely did anything but work. Yet he spoke as if he understood the crippling agony that captured his own heart. Not that he would concede such a thing to love. "Do ye?"

Logan's jaw stiffened, a grim smile coming across it. "Aye, plenty."

Finn dragged a hand through his hair and let it rest on the back of his neck. If Logan noticed his behaviour, surely others had, including Katelyn. He needed to find a way to regain his composure, remind himself why he avoided women. Strange how the memories of Alice's death—the cries of pain, the pale skin, the tiny bundle beside her, so quiet and still—was muted in Katelyn's presence. These recollections no longer shadowed him.

But only with her.

Now they were fresh and raw, and stabbing his fragile heart.

He did what he did best. He flicked on a grin and slapped a hand to Logan's back. "Have no fear, friend, ye'll no' catch me falling in love any time soon. And certainly not with the bride of Laird Gillean."

***

The faery stomped her feet against the wooden railing of the gallery and huffed. By the stars, it was all going wrong. Hurt swam in Catriona's eyes as Finn's declaration rang out through the hall, no doubt made louder by those two beakers of ale he'd consumed.

Now Catriona *had* to be convinced there was no future for them. And at this rate there really wouldn't be. Laird Gillean was on his way. She could delay him with yet more weather spells or ask for help from the nymphs but she was meant to do this alone and keep her magic to a minimum. What if she messed with fate again? She'd never return home.

Catriona spun and hid herself in her room. Tèile tapped her foot, crossing her arms. Two days? It wasn't enough. Three days and they were destined to come together properly. How much could a faery do with such limited powers?

Her wings sagged. This was all going to be for nothing. And the idea that maybe she wouldn't get to return home wasn't the only thing that bothered her. She scowled. These two people might miss their chance at happiness and for some reason that really anguished her.

CHAPTER SIX

With one day before Laird Gillean's anticipated arrival, the need for escape struck. Despair beat heavily in Catriona's chest as she hurried out of the castle walls and onto the surrounding peaks. She paused and glanced at the keep, nestled so perfectly in the dips between the yellow-green hills, and sucked in a breath. Releasing her skirts, she dropped to sit, closed her eyes, tilted her head to the sky and enjoyed the pricking warmth of the sun on her skin. She needed a few moments of freedom. A little time not having to play a part. Of not suffering heartache every time Finn came near.

She rested her head on her knees and wrapped her arms around them. What to do now? Wait and pray her father arrived? Admit the truth? Go ahead and marry the laird and hope he did not take his anger out on her when her true identity came to light? Which it would. Eventually.

All yesterday, the desire to spill out everything to Lorna

raged inside. The woman was kind and caring, but this was not her fight and Gillean was her kin by marriage. Lorna's duty was to the man who was her overlord first. She refused to risk Lorna getting involved. She suspected the woman would gladly stand at her side and demand Gillean cease his attentions toward Bute but where would that leave Lorna? Her home and future depended on Gillean.

Her only other choice was Finn. The man who had dismissed her so easily. She'd been right in the first place. He felt nothing more than a passing fancy for her. Simple, masculine lust. How foolish she had been to read anything more into it. Catriona snorted to herself. She could not blame him. Who would want a woman plagued by demons? One who was betrothed at that. She should not be hurt by his dismissal. After all, he was clearly the only one with any sense.

A prickle skipped along her spine and she drew her head up. Oh Lord, not him. Of all people, did it have to be Finn?

With a strong and steady gait, he strode up the hill, purpose written on his face. She heard his heavy breaths as he came to her side. He snatched her arm and hauled her to her feet.

"What in the devil are ye doing out here alone?"

She fought his hold, heart pounding—not from fear but from surprise. His glowering expression chilled her. "What are ye doing, Finn?"

"Ye..." He grabbed her other arm as she wriggled and pinned her flat against his chest. "Damnation, keep still! We didnae know where ye were. *Keep* still!" he said through a clenched jaw.

"Release me," she demanded, panting from exertion and the crush of his body.

"By God, lass, do ye not know how dangerous it is to be out alone? In yer state too?"

Catriona froze. "What do ye mean?"

He glowered at her while his fingers dug into her upper arms. "I dinnae know what yer capable of right now. Not after...."

"I wouldnae harm myself!"

"Well, I didnae know that, did I? Hell's teeth, Katie, Lorna's had her men searching the keep top to bottom. I thought...."

"What?"

"I thought ye could be dead!"

He said it with such sincerity, such concern, she almost believed he cared. Mayhap he did purely because he'd yet to tumble her. But the anguish flickering in his gaze pulled roughly at her heart. Drawing her chin up, she vowed not to succumb to such weak emotions. She'd spent enough time feeling fragile and helpless.

"Why should ye care?"

"Why should I...?" he spluttered. "Ye surely are the most confusing, aggravating, troublesome lass I have ever met."

"Ach, if ye came out here to insult me, ye can turn around and leave me now." She flattened her palms against his chest in a bid to push him away but all it succeeded in doing was make her aware of the sinuous muscle and strong heartbeat beneath the linen.

"Ye scared me, Katie," he ground out, "and I'll no' have ye do it again. I'll no' be scared by a woman again."

With savage speed, his mouth came down upon hers. She made a sound as he pressed his lips forcefully to hers. Fingers curled into his shirt, she sagged as heat speared straight to her core. This aggressive, demanding kiss threatened to turn her legs to oil.

Deep down, the fight in her ignited. She would not crumble or succumb to weakness. Instead, she flattened her aching breasts to him and gripped tighter. When she opened her mouth to his searching tongue, he groaned—the sound sending thrills skittering through her. He still had her arms in a strong hold but it did not hurt—only made her feel safe and resilient, as if Finn's strength fed into her. In his arms, she was no longer a damaged woman, haunted by demons. She was a woman, flesh and blood. Wanted and needed. Even if only for a quick bedding.

His tongue searched her mouth and clashed with hers.

Catriona met him, kiss for kiss, driven by a need for more. More sensation, a deeper taste. More Finn. His arousal prodded her stomach and her mind drifted, filled with images of naked flesh and pleasure.

Something broke the heat—a spatter of rain drops and Finn jerked away. His ragged breaths blew over her, his chest heaved and she gulped. She missed his warmth but the look in his eyes... had she been wrong? He searched her gaze desperately for something.

He still had hold of her arms and he placed her back, took a step away and scraped a hand through his hair. "Forgive me, wee lass, that was...."

"A mistake?"

"Aye, nay, I..." He dropped his head briefly only to reveal a wide grin when he lifted it. "Ye'll forgive me, lass. What can I say? Too much ale mayhap." He reached for her. "Come, let us get ye back to the keep."

Catriona shook her head vigorously and folded her arms. She recognised that grin. He used it often. But she'd never noticed how deliberately he used if before. It was disarming and he knew it. Used to send her off track. He'd been about to say something, intended to reveal more, but he'd snapped on that smile and covered it. What else did he cover like that? How many other hurts did he conceal with such a look? Mayhap she was not the only one hiding.

"Can we no' stay a little longer?" She glanced up at the skies and frowned. The heavens were clear aside from a few puffy white clouds. The threat of rain had passed in an instant. Strange. She turned an imploring look on Finn. "Just a wee while longer. I need some fresh air. Ye know I dinnae do well in castle walls."

His shoulders dropped and he nodded slowly. "Just a wee while. Lorna shall be worrying for ye."

Sitting, Catriona curled her legs to one side and patted the ground in invitation. "I didnae mean to worry anyone. I just needed some air. I didnae think anyone would notice. I intended to use the passageway when I returned in the hope that I could sneak in and no one would be any the wiser."

Logan had revealed the escape passage through the back of the keep on her first day. He told her it was intended for times of war. Why he showed her, she knew not. She suspected Logan was the kind of man who planned for every eventuality.

Finn sat beside her, drawing one knee up and resting an elbow on it. He stared out over the hills, affording her the chance to appreciate his profile.

"Did ye truly think I wouldnae notice?"

She rested her chin on her knees. "Aye."

"Ye dinnae know me well at all," he concluded.

She tilted her head to view him, cheek supported by her knee. "I dinnae think anyone knows ye well, Finn," she replied softly. "But I am learning."

Finn's throat flexed and his great body heaved with a sigh. "Ye are too canny for yer own good, Katie."

"I dinnae think anyone has ever called me canny."

"Then they dinnae know *ye*."

"But ye do?"

He gave a half shrug and shifted. "Well enough."

Here, she suspected, was the real Finn. The tender and open one. There were no quick smiles or chuckles. She'd seen glimpses of him in his care of her but this was the first time she'd had a conversation with him. She wouldn't give up that chance. Curiosity forced the next question from her lips.

"Did yer wife know ye well?"

A muscle in his jaw ticked and he remained focused ahead, as if scouting the land for enemy. "How do ye know of her?"

"Lorna told me a little. Not much."

"Lorna shouldnae be speaking of such things."

"Why? I am yer friend, am I not? At least I thought I was. We spoke of many things on our journey yet ye never mentioned Alice."

The tiniest ripple of his muscles suggested he'd shuddered. Had she pushed too far? Telling Finn of her troubles had eased her dreams and she had not swooned since. She longed to offer him the same comfort.

"'Twas a long time ago.

"Ye told me I should speak of my troubles. Do ye no' think ye should take yer own advice?" She plucked a strand of grass from her skirt and fingered it. "Did ye love her?" she prompted, bracing herself for the answer. As much as he needed to speak of it, him loving another made her stomach churn with jealousy. Not that it should. Finn had made no declarations toward her.

"Aye." Finn twisted to look at her. "Aye, in a way. We were young. She was a good woman. I have heard the bards speak of love and I dinnae think it was that, but I loved her in my own way, aye."

"I am sorry." She reached over and rested her hand on top of the one at his side. He didn't take her hand as she had hoped but he did not move either.

"Sometimes I wonder if I do not love the memory of her more." He shook his head. "But 'tis no matter. This is all in the past."

"The past shapes us, Finn."

He chuckled, admiration in his expression. "And ye say ye are not canny? Lass, yer surely the canniest woman I know." Before she responded, he snatched her hand and came to his feet, taking her with him. "Come, let us return before my sister tears apart the castle."

Catriona peered sideways at him, her heart heavy. That

grin was back in place. He'd hidden himself away again. Still, she would treasure the trust he had put in her, even if it was only brief. And she would try not to read too much into it. She had other things to worry about. Like the fact her dead sister's betrothed would be arriving on the morrow.

***

Gillean arrived in a fanfare of horses, banners and too much fuss in Finn's opinion. He folded his arms, widened his stance and drew in a breath through his nostrils as the laird discarded his mantle and dipped to kiss Lorna's hand. Lorna smiled but Finn saw tension in her posture while she greeted him at the large oak doors.

The man breezed in—as if he owned the place. Which, of course, he did. Finn mentally kicked himself and forced his glower to relax. Stood in front of the top table, he had a good view of everything. Including Katelyn's discomfiture as Lorna introduced her and Gillean's gaze roamed over Katelyn, no doubt weighing her up and finding her more than satisfactory.

Finn couldn't hear what either of them said but he knew well what Gillean would be thinking. He'd be congratulating himself on winning such a prize. In a deep purple gown that reminded him of heather after rainfall, her skin glowed and her hair shone. She'd clearly taken extra effort to dress for the laird and that made Finn grind his teeth until his jaw hurt.

When Gillean took Katelyn's hand and dropped a lingering kiss to it, Finn had to lean against one of the candle mounts and grip it. The iron dug into his palm but at least he wasn't ploughing his fist into the smug laird's face.

Gillean finally turned his attention away from Katelyn and offered Finn a smile. An understanding ran between them, one that acknowledged Gillean had won, even though Gillean had no way of knowing how he felt about Katelyn.

How did he feel about Katelyn?

Ach, he was imagining things. He wasn't in competition with Gillean.

"Finn, how goes it?" Gillean strode over and dropped his head briefly.

"Well enough," he replied tightly. He had not seen Gillean for many years. Gillean had been old enough when his brother had married Lorna but his hair was now completely white and deep lines framed his grey eyes. A thick white beard barely concealed his smirk.

"Lorna tells me I have ye to thank for rescuing Lady Katelyn." He glanced over at her and motioned for her to come to him. With slow movements, she came to his side and slipped her hand into his offered one.

Finn released the iron mount and flexed his fist at his side. Katelyn refused to look at him. Her gaze remained cast down, studying the reed-strewn floorboards with great interest.

"If ye had sent more men, I wouldnae have had to."

Gillean's eyes narrowed marginally before he let out a laugh. "Alas, when I travel I have a need for many men. I doubt anyone would attack ye, Finn. Not when there would be little benefit in it for them."

Finn bit back a growl and Katelyn snapped her head up, swinging her wide gaze between them. Swallowing his resentment, Finn gave him a mocking bow. "I am but yer servant, my laird, and I cannae object to aiding a beloved sister. Should she have been without any more men, I would have feared for her safety, and of course the safety of yer castle. I fear ye have too many enemies, Gillean, to leave it unmanned so," Finn said pointedly.

"Ha, none would be foolish enough to attack my property." He squeezed Katelyn's hand. "Finn here would have ye believe ye would be in great danger as my wife, but let me assure ye, my lady, ye will come to no harm by my side. I am greatly feared across the Highlands."

"Aye, that I know," she said quietly, but Finn heard the bitterness in her tone and scowled.

"None would go against me," Gillean continued, ignoring or mayhap not even hearing Katelyn's soft statement.

Lorna approached, a warning look in her eyes. "Ye must be worn from yer journey, will ye no' take some refreshments,

Gillean?" She motioned to the laid table behind her.

"Aye, thank ye, sister. It has been a long few sennights, but I believe I have made some fine business arrangements."

Finn barely smothered a snort. Business deals? If the man counted threats as arrangements, mayhap. He was willing to bet Gillean had never made an honourable deal in his life.

The laird turned to Katelyn. "Will ye do me the honour of allowing me to serve ye, my lady."

"Of course, my laird."

"Pray, call me Gillean. I would not have one of those marriages where we stand upon ceremony."

"Gillean then."

The laird's name coming from her lips sent bile into Finn's throat. Disgusted, he snatched a cup and a jug of ale. "If ye'll excuse me, I must see to something."

Gillean did not even acknowledge Finn's words, his attention consumed by Katelyn as he saw her to her seat and placed himself next to her. Finn could well understand his enchantment. Finn had suffered the same ever since he first met her, but did he have to look at her with such obvious lust?

"Forgive me, sister," he murmured to Lorna. "I shall see ye at supper."

Lorna gave a resigned sigh and patted his arm in understanding. "Aye, as ye will."

Before he stormed out of the hall, he glanced at Katelyn. She sat rigid, only the ghost of a smile on her lips while Gillean offered her a fig. He fed it to her and Finn's throat burned. He turned away and pushed through the oak doors. Had he seen what he thought he had in Katelyn's eyes? He scrubbed a hand across his jaw. A plea for help had lingered in those green eyes and by God, he wanted to answer it.

***

Finn threw back his wine and got up to pour some more. He scowled as his chambers wobbled and he had to steady himself against the wall.

Snatching the pitcher from the bedside table, he poured himself a hearty drink and paused to gaze out of the window. The evening had grown dark and many would be abed. Clouds covered the stars this night. He snorted. Appropriate. The darkness mirrored his mood. He sucked in the fresh air but it did little to cool the bubbling anger inside.

All supper he'd suffered observing Gillean's fawning and touching, watched his arrogance and listened to his boasts. While Lorna pandered to him, Katelyn remained reserved, smiling and commenting quietly at the right moments. Mayhap only he saw the fear in her eyes. And it seemed like more than that of a maiden set to marry a man of which she knew nothing. He closed his eyes and leaned against the wall.

The tension in the keep was unbearable. He understood Katelyn's need to escape. How he longed to do so. Lorna had retreated to bed with dark shadows under her eyes and grim strain in the lines around her mouth. He had done her no favours leaving her to deal with Gillean all afternoon. He opened his eyes and thrust a hand into his hair. Ach, he'd failed her yet again. When would he cease letting down the women in his life? Put a sword in his hand and fear deserted him but it was the unseen dangers that terrified him. Illness, childbirth. Ach, women were such delicate creatures. How could a man invest his emotions in a lass when they were so easily taken away? Even his own sister.

He would change that though. Hadn't he already sworn to be a better brother to her? He'd confront Gillean about his choice of husband for her and ensure she had a good match. She needed someone by her side. As bold as she was, the strain of running a castle alone was too much for a lass to cope with. He would at least have her looked after by a good man.

On the morrow he intended to make up for his behaviour. But for now, he would drink. He grinned. Aye, drink to forget. That always helped. Forget Lorna and Alice and the babe. Just for one night. Forget Katelyn....

Discarding the beaker on the window ledge, he reached for the jug of wine. He cursed as he stumbled and knocked the cup out the window. He peered over but darkness swallowed it. Damnation. He traipsed out of his room, pausing in his doorway as he heard voices.

Logan.

Finn couldn't hear what was being said but he stood in the entrance to Lorna's solar. Feminine whispers reached his ears and he clenched a fist. Why did Logan visit his sister's chambers so late at night? He stared hard and saw the flash of a white chemise. The door slammed shut suddenly and Logan cursed aloud before turning away. Finn dropped into the shadows of his room as Logan stormed by, adjusting his plaid.

Shaking his head in disgust, Finn clenched his jaw tight and fisted a hand at his side. With bed-rumpled hair and garments in disarray, Finn had a fine idea of what Logan had been doing. The swine. The bastard. He'd trusted Logan to look after his sister, not *bed* her.

He stormed after him, barrelling down the stairs and out of the hall. He spilled out onto the rough ground and groaned. Pulling himself to standing, he took a moment to get his bearings and gave a mocking laugh. Logan was nowhere to be seen. A small mercy, given Finn's drunken state.

He perched on the remains of the low stone wall that had been replaced by the larger one and chugged what wine hadn't spilled from the jug. He peered around. Only a few men remained on the walls, their footsteps quiet. Finally he felt free of Katelyn. She was everywhere. Not that he had seen her since supper, but everywhere he went, her face teased his mind. If he looked at the stairs, he remembered her climbing them. When he set foot in his chambers, he imagined her on his bed. Even escaping to the kitchens didn't help. All he could think of was throwing her up onto that large table in the middle, parting her thighs and losing himself.

With a laugh, he shook his head and drank the last remaining drops of wine. He'd spent all day avoiding her when all he longed to do was fold her into his embrace and protect her from everything. In his gut that familiar dread churned but he ignored it. Just because he cared for her welfare, did not mean he cared for *her*. It did not mean he had any attachment to her. Hadn't he learned it was dangerous to care for a woman? Life was too risky, especially for the lasses. He would never go through that kind of grief again. His interest in Katelyn was as a friend and that of a brother to Lorna. Lorna needed his aid so he would give it.

Never mind that she'd been the only woman he'd ever opened up to about Alice. He shook away the memories. Lord, that woman sent him out of his wits—more addictive and dangerous than a poppy tonic. She addled his mind. What nonsense had he said about love? How he thought mayhap he loved the memory of Alice more than he'd really loved Alice? Had that been true? Was he so determined to cling to the hurt that he couldn't remember how he'd actually felt about Alice?

When he looked at Katelyn, his love for Alice seemed so insipid—a young, foolish kind of love. As sweet and as lovely as she was, Finn had never felt the same desperate need for her as he did Katelyn.

Footsteps drew his attention. Logan stepped out of the hall, glanced around and ran a hand through his brown hair. Jaw tense, Finn narrowed his eyes and studied the man. He must have gone to the armoury. His sister trusted Logan unquestionably. Was she also trusting him with her body? A swell of anger made is skin hot. He did not like the idea of the man putting his hands on Lorna. She was still vulnerable after her marriage to her controlling husband. He could hardly stand by and let someone take his pleasure and bring shame on Lorna.

"Logan!" he shouted and came unsteadily to his feet. He dropped the jug, not caring when he heard a crack. "Logan," he said again when the man turned to face him. "I crave a word with ye."

"What can I do for ye, Finn?"

In the glowing torch light, Logan's strong features looked strained and tired. Good. Let that be his punishment for believing he could take advantage of his sister.

"I saw ye leaving Lorna's chambers."

Logan seemed to take a moment to consider this before nodding. "Aye, ye may have done."

Finn curled his hand into a fist. Ach, the man did not even dispute it. Did he boast with his men of bedding the lady of the keep? Damn him.

"So ye dinnae deny it?"

"I dinnae deny it," he replied evenly. "I am in no habit of lying to ye, Finn."

Rage bubbled up inside Finn and he breathed heavily through his nostrils. The gall of the man. Looking him straight in the eyes and calmly declaring he'd bedded his sister! Before he realised what he'd done, he brought a fist across Logan's face.

The man staggered back, eyes wide. When he didn't fall, it only incensed Finn more. Why did he not even show the slightest bit of shame? He had thought Logan honourable. Hell, he'd trusted him with his sister.

Leaping forward, Finn used his weight to push Logan to the ground. Instead of fighting him, Logan held up his fists in defence and tried to shove him off. Finn was too heavy and used the chance to punch his undefended ribs. The brown haired man expelled a gagging cough and Finn repeated the movement. Blood trickled from Logan's nose.

With a sudden show of strength, Logan used his feet to propel Finn away. It took Finn by surprise and he ended up pinned underneath the man. The wine must have dulled his senses as, though Logan was a strong man, no one could defeat

Finn in a fair fight. He stared up at Logan while the man kept him restrained with an arm across his neck. He braced himself for a hit, but none came.

"I dinnae blame ye for yer anger." Logan drew in a ragged breath. "But 'tis misplaced. Ye should know better than anyone I wouldnae harm yer sister."

Finn narrowed his eyes and shoved Logan away. Logan allowed him to clamber to his feet and eyed him warily.

"If ye want to look after her, ye willnae bed her again."

"I make no promises." Logan crossed his arms over his chest.

With a roar, Finn ran for Logan again but a blinding pain struck him across the mouth and he realised he'd run into a fist. He reeled back, a hand to his now bloody lip.

"I love her," Logan said quietly as Finn tried to blink away the painful haze the punch had left him with. "I fear 'twill come to naught but I willnae make a promise I dinnae intend to keep. If I can persuade Lorna she loves me too then any promise would be for naught."

Finn let his shoulders drop. Ach, he was a fool. He should have known Logan would have honourable intentions. The man admired his sister more than anyone. Of course he loved her. Anyone could see that. Apart from him apparently. When exactly did he become the fool? If anyone had dishonourable intentions it was him. But no longer. Nay, he was determined to be as chivalrous as Logan.

"I wish ye luck...."

"What are ye doing, ye great fools?" A feminine voice cut him off and he saw Katelyn stood at the top of the steps to the kitchens.

Logan held up his hands. "Dinnae worry, my lady, all is settled now, is it not?" He looked at Finn for confirmation.

"Aye, all is settled."

With a nod, Logan retreated into the hall. Finn pitied him really. Finn knew no one more stubborn than his sister. He'd have a hard time convincing her of his love.

The word lingering in this mind—*love*—he faced Katelyn. Hands on her hips, chin set into a determined thrust, he braced himself for a scolding.

"What were ye doing? Have ye been fighting? One of the maids ran down and said Logan had ye pinned to the ground." She sniffed as she approached. "Have ye been drinking?"

Finn grimaced. "Aye, just a wee drop."

She froze and her gaze lingered on his mouth. Cursing inwardly, he put his hand to his lip. No doubt the sight of blood summoned many horrific memories. Hell, the sight of him acting like a barbarian did not likely help either.

Shoulders straight, she reached for his hand and drew it away. The tiniest flicker of uncertainty dashed across her face and he heard her suck in a breath. She touched his lip and he held back a wince.

"Let's clean this up," she ordered and snatched his hand.

Her small, cool fingers in his sent a tremor up his arm and he gulped. She dragged him down the stairs to the kitchen. It was empty save for one maid who excused herself upon seeing them. A few candles flickered on the side tables but everything had been cleared away for the night, apart from a pestle and mortar and a few leaves. Bunches of herbs hung from a metal rack above the table, scenting the air.

"What were ye doing in here, lass?"

Katelyn grinned and held up a pot. "Preparing a yarrow root salve." She motioned to a stool and made him sit. Her smile dropped as she scooped some out with her finger and shuffled closer. "'Tis for scratches and... and bruises."

The foggy haze from the wine dissipated a little and he furrowed his brow. "Ye have need of it?"

"I..." She licked her lips. "'Tis naught. Just a few wee scratches. It happens when I... ye know...."

"When ye have those dreams?"

"Aye."

"Ye still suffer?"

"Sometimes. Though not as badly as before." Katelyn's mesmerising gaze latched onto his for the merest instant before dropping to his lips. "'Tis no matter." She dabbed a dollop of the salve on his lips and its sweet fragrance teased.

"It does matter, Katie." He tried to focus on her face and not on the hint of rounded breasts that sat in his eye line, still encased in that deep purple. The balm stung but Katelyn's beautiful figure made him forget it. He dragged his gaze up. "I dinnae like the thought of ye coming to harm."

"Ach, a few scratches and bruises… 'tis nothing to be concerned about."

She drew her hand away from his lip and hooked a finger under his chin to inspect the damage. "Why were ye fighting, Finn?"

"Because I am a fool," he offered with a tilted grin.

"Yer no fool." Katelyn dropped her hand and backed away. "But ye are drunk. What did Logan do to anger ye?"

"He loves my sister."

"And why does that anger ye?"

Finn laughed. "I told ye, I am a fool. I was a fool with ye and a fool with Logan."

"Why were ye a fool with me?"

Curses, this would not do. He stood abruptly, making her stumble and he hooked an arm around her waist to prevent her from falling. She was soft and giving in his arms, even with plenty of space between them.

"Ye make it hard for me to be an honourable man," he murmured.

He saw her throat work when she gulped and her hands

slid up his arms. "Ye dinnae need to be honourable, Finn. I dinnae ask anything of ye. Ye...ye make me feel safe. Ye scared away the demons somehow. I think yer a very special man."

"I cannae dishonour ye." His voice came out tight while she continued to work her hands up and down his arms. His skin tingled wherever she touched.

Something clouded her eyes. Uncertainty mayhap? Fear? By God, he did not want her scared. He tugged her near, remembering how his body seemed to soothe her. The look—that haunted, troubled one—dissolved, leaving expectant breaths and eyes that darkened with need. Katelyn lifted her chin and clutched his neck, pressing her hands underneath his hair. He used his free hand to clasp her close, splaying it over the curve of her rear.

They shared several breaths as she raised herself up and he savoured them. When was the last time he'd enjoyed simply holding a woman. He couldn't remember. With Alice mayhap? Nay, not even then. Before he could think further, he closed the gap and his body came instantly alive at the feeling of velvety lips beneath his.

Katelyn trembled in his arms and parted her lips allowing access. And though he'd intended to take it slow—ach, he'd not intended to kiss her at all—her taste drove the very sense from him. One touch of her tongue and he took everything she could give. Each thrust of her tongue, each sigh and desperate touch made him hunger for her. But he could not take her.

To give her pleasure though… surely that was not such a dishonourable act?

He bunched her skirts in his hand, fingers brushing the smooth skin of her thigh and his knees threatened to buckle beneath him. Finn ached. Unbelievably so. But the agony would be nothing if he could but banish some of Katelyn's torment. Now was not the time for battle or strong words. At a loss for any other way to combat it, he would use softer methods. As he kissed her, an intense, mind-numbing kiss, then manoeuvred her toward the table and lifted her. Katelyn kept her hold on his neck, apparently unwilling to release him. Her skirts remained up around her thighs giving him easy access. He broke their kiss for the briefest moment to admire her. Dishevelled hair, glossy eyes, crumpled skirts, unreasonably lush lips… His knees juddered again and he plunged a hand between her legs at the same time as gripping the back of her neck to take her mouth once more.

Heat and dampness greeted his fingers, the scent of arousal pervaded the air. He longed to draw it in, the fragrance of his sweet, sweet Katie, but alas that delicious mouth of hers would not let him. She wriggled against his fingers, begged incoherently for more, her words drowned by the forceful movements of his lips.

Legs shaking, Katelyn rocked into his hand and he circled

her folds before plunging two fingers inside her. She cried out against his mouth, the sound gripping his heart. To bring Katelyn pleasure had to be the most rewarding experience of his life. He couldn't think of a single lover who compared to her. Her open response, her delicious taste and fragrance—none could possibly compare.

Her thighs tensed and she was close. He pressed harder—with determination. Voices filtered down from outside and they both stiffened.

Gillean. And Logan, he assumed.

"Have ye seen Lady Katelyn?"

"Nay, my laird," Logan replied.

Finn resumed his movements and she released a suppressed cry. Finn pressed his lips to Katelyn's ear. "Hush."

"I assumed she was abed but her chamber door is open," Gillean continued.

"Forgive me, my laird, I havenae seen her. Mayhap she is praying?"

"This late at night?" the laird sneered.

Forcefully, Finn worked in and out of her. He would bring her such pleasure that her worries would be driven from her mind and replaced by memories of what he did to her. Even when she was married to Gillean, she'd remember him. And, by God, would he remember it too. He never wanted to forget the day Katelyn came apart in his arms.

"The kitchens mayhap?" Logan offered.

Heart pounding, he let his lips linger on her cheek as her breaths came in frantic gasps and she dropped her hands to grip at the top of his arms. He retreated further so as to watch it happen. It would take a whole army to prevent him from seeing this. Gillean certainly wouldn't. Eyes wide, lips parted, she tensed. Her gaze never left his. The lass was braver than she realised. She didn't hide any of it. He watched the gratification flow through her, clear in her eyes while she pulsed around him. Her legs dropped, she sagged and rested her forehead flat against his chest.

Finn withdrew slowly and fisted his hand, using the other to stroke the back of her neck. Katelyn gathered her breath and finally lifted her head. Her grateful smile made his insides squeeze.

A creak. A footstep. Finn jumped away and helped Katelyn off the table. She hurriedly rearranged her skirts as Gillean ducked into the kitchen, peering about the dim room with a raised brow.

"Lady Katelyn, what are ye doing in here?"

The smell of arousal lingered in the air. Gillean had to smell it. Finn peeked at Katelyn and saw her throat work. Hell fire, had he ruined her chances of marriage? What had he been thinking?

He hadn't.

"I was tending to Finn," she said suddenly and smoothly. "As ye can see," she motioned to his lip, "he has harmed himself."

Gillean peered at Finn who clenched his jaw. He'd all but forgotten his lip. Nodding, Gillean released a slow smile, one that reminded Finn of a wolf about to pounce on his prey.

"Careless, Finn." He clicked his tongue and turned to Katelyn. "Ye are a caring lass it seems, but he is a grown man. I am sure he can tend to himself. 'Tis late. Can I not escort ye to yer chambers?" He offered an arm and Finn clenched the edge of the table to keep from snapping that arm off.

Katelyn remained calm. Though heat still showed in her cheeks and the tiniest bead of perspiration sat in the dip of her neck—and how he longed to lap at it—she appeared serene. He envied her composure. He throbbed with unspent tension and simmering fury. All had been so perfect until Gillean had interrupted.

She nodded and took Gillean's arm. "I bid ye good night, Finn," she said over her shoulder. Only he could have caught the flash of sorrow in her dazzling eyes. None knew her like he did.

"Good eve, Katelyn." By some miracle, he managed to sound formal.

He eyed their progress up the stairs and slumped against the table when they were out of sight, both hands thrust into his hair. What had he done? Her fragrance—lavender and desire even cut through the herby air of the kitchen. Likely, he'd remember it forever. But soon enough Gillean would be the one enjoying it and where would that leave him? He had to push her out of his mind. He had nothing to offer—a distrusting broken man was no better than Laird Gillean. He slammed a fist into the wooden table. He had to conquer this need for her. What other choice did he have?

***

The woman slept silently as Tèile fluttered over her. She studied Katelyn's relaxed features. Interesting, no need for dreams here. She already dreamed of Finn. Tèile scratched her head. Things had gone so very wrong. None of it was going according to plan and while they were clearly made for one another, too many outside influences had got in the way. Tèile was at a loss as to what to do. The *sidhe* council would be furious but as much as the council liked to think they knew everything, they never quite understood the workings of the human heart. So often, they went against their fate. It frustrated most faeries but she reckoned she had a better understanding than most. So much time in the mortal realm had taught her plenty, she thought with a huff.

She settled on the pillow next to Katelyn's head. It was the first time she'd been able to rest with Katelyn. Normally the woman tossed and turned so much Tèile risked being hit or squashed. But Finn's attentions had soothed her nightmares. Very interesting.

It was no good. She'd have to do something big. Something that would take some proper magic. She looked forward to dusting off her fingers but the risk was great. Fate could change yet again. Still, she was a green faery. Meddling was what she did. Soon she'd have this wrapped up and she could return and truly celebrate her success.

Her grin expanded when she considered how the council would react. They never really had faith in her matchmaking abilities. If she hadn't been just a little bit naughty and played a few jokes on some of the council members, they never would have sent her here.

But she'd show them....

CHAPTER SEVEN

Stretching, Katelyn sucked in a breath and opened her eyes. She sat up abruptly when she noted the flickers of daylight seeping in through the shutters. Sweet Mary, she'd slept all night. She lifted the blankets and her chemise to study her legs. No bruises or scratches.

A hand to her lips, she felt their puffiness as she recalled the previous evening. All her dreams had been of Finn. The man had practically taken over her thoughts. Without a doubt her good night's sleep had been down to him.

She sighed and climbed out of bed, padding across the cold wooden floor to the washbowl in front of the windows. Mae must have already been in. Clean garments and water awaited her. Katelyn flung open the shutters, pleased to note the day was fresh but clear skied. The clean scent of a new day and nature greeted her and she drew it in, chest rising with a deep inhale.

Washing quickly, she rubbed herself down with a cloth and wrapped the linen about herself. The dress Mae had placed out for her needed lacing at the back and it would be difficult to do herself. She shrugged. She'd manage though.

Linen clutched around her, she turned her attention to the open window. Several stories up, she had a good view of the surrounding countryside. Grey rocks sprouted from the ground like wild flowers and sheep mingled amongst them.

The men strode about the bailey below and she searched hard for Finn but saw no sign of his fair head and wide shoulders. Ach, she had so hoped to catch sight of him before running into him again. The previous evening had astounded her. Never before had she felt such a need for a man. Never longed for someone with a craving that made her ache all over. She needed more.

Not that she could have more. Finn was still in love with his wife and hadn't he declared he would never fall for her? Why did she long for someone who likely only had a passing fancy for her body? Not to mention they'd nearly been caught by Laird Gillean. If he suspected anything, he never said so. Bute's fate rested on her shoulders and she would do well to remember that. More was at stake than her overwhelming desire for Finn.

"Catriona, ye are wanton," she told herself. She wasn't sure when that had happened. When had she become so needy?

She slipped into her chemise and fought with her gown. She managed to do it up though probably not tightly enough. Presumably Mae had not wished to disturb her. The thoughtfulness of the maid made her smile, reminding her of her friends at home. She ran a comb through her hair and used a red ribbon to tie it into a simple braid. Picking up the polished metal mirror, she grimaced. Attractive enough, aye, but not nearly as elegant compared to the previous day. But without Mae's help she could do no better and she did not need to attract more attention from Gillean.

She shuddered, recalling stony grey eyes and lingering touches—wildly inappropriate even if they were to be married. If her father were here he would never allow such behaviour. Catriona recalled Gillean's cold lips on her hands and the times he'd managed to touch her, even accidentally grazing her breasts or thighs. She snorted inwardly. No doubt those accidental touches were deliberate. She'd seen that look many times and it was so very far removed from one of genuine desire and... and love?

Shaking the thought of blue eyes that *did* hold such a look—no matter how much she told herself it meant nothing—she drew up her chin and slid her feet into her dainty silk slippers. Today she needed to find a way to delay the wedding, and maintain her resolve. With a good night's sleep behind her she felt better able to deal with whatever Gillean threw at her. Mayhap she could also persuade Lorna to send a messenger to Bute or the coast to find out what was happening.

Aye. She allowed herself a smile. It would take a messenger four days or so to get to the shoreline if he were fast. If she delayed things a wee while longer, she could send word to her father and beg for his rescue. Surely he had never intended for her to be gone this long?

A few sprigs of lavender remained on her side table so she snatched them and rubbed them against her wrists and neck before straightening her skirts. Inwardly, she steeled herself. Mayhap she shouldn't have given into her needs the previous evening but it had given her much courage. Her bold actions had cracked through some of her fear and muted the memories. No longer did she remember filthy Viking hands. They were replaced with Finn's knowing fingers.

The morning meal was under way by the time she came out of her chambers and descended the stairs. Gillean sat in Finn's usual seat, with Finn perched on the end, shoulders slumped, hair slightly rumpled, as were his garments.

Catriona came around behind him, barely resisting the urge to stroke her hand over his back, and seated herself next to Gillean. The laird watched her—she felt his gaze even as she tried to avoid it.

"Good morrow, my lady."

"Good morrow, my laird."

"Ye must call me Gillean."

He wanted to call her Katelyn—that was what he was hinting at—but she couldn't bring herself to give him permission. She assumed he would take the liberty soon enough. Why it mattered, she knew not. It was not even her name, but it kept one small barrier erected between them.

"Did ye sleep well?" he persisted as she poured a cup of ale and a servant piled her platter with fruit, cheese and sliced pork.

"Aye, well, thank ye."

"Good. We have much to arrange this day. Lorna tells me yer gown is nearly ready and I have summoned a priest."

This was her chance. She licked her lips. "I... I was hoping my father could be present before we said our vows." She kept her gaze on the pewter plate in front of her.

"I see," he said tightly. A hand grazed her thigh and then boldly curled around it. She gasped and met his gaze, eyes wide. "I imagine yer father is taken up with the attack on Bute, is he not?"

"I... I dinnae know." Something malicious sat in his eyes. Did he know? Iciness seeped into her, chilling to the core. "He said he wished to be here for such a joyous union," she lied.

He pursed his lips, as if considering her words. Deciding if they were the truth?

"We have a few days yet. If he is not here by then, then we can delay no longer. My lands have been untended for too long. And, of course, I am most keen to make ye my wife." He gave her leg another squeeze, a hard one this time and she bit down on her lip.

Had that been a threat? A warning? She could not make the man out. She nodded slowly. A few days would not be long enough. She needed to find another way to delay. Or else... or else she could run, but what of Bute? She would be better marrying him and hoping her father came to her rescue. If he even bothered. Mayhap he had decided to leave her to her fate. She'd assumed his ambitions for her sister would be transferred over to her upon her death but mayhap he thought her a lost cause by now.

The strength and determination she'd felt earlier was slipping away.

Her hands grew shaky and it took all her concentration to keep her food on her eating knife. If she married Gillean, he would be no better than the Norseman.

Catriona ate little and only relaxed once the servants began clearing away the plates and scraps. She managed to attract Lorna's attention as she stood and they met near the empty fire pit.

The fair haired woman looked her up and down, a furrow between her brows. "Katelyn, is all well?"

"Aye, well enough." She'd barely spoken to Lorna since she'd revealed Finn's past to her. The lady had grown quiet of late. Something plagued her. Catriona longed to ask more but what advice could she offer? "Lorna, would ye be able to send a messenger to Bute? Or the villages on the coast? He might be seeking sanctuary there if Bute was overrun."

"Aye, that should be possible. I am surprised we've not had word from there yet but I assumed yer father has likely had his hands full with the invasion."

"I would be pleased to hear how things are and to let him know that I may be wed by the time I see him next."

"Indeed, ye may well be." Lorna smiled tightly. "Write a missive and I shall send my fastest rider."

"I thank ye, Lorna. Ye have been so very kind to me, as have yer men."

She waved a hand. "I am just doing my duty, Katelyn."

"Aye, but ye have done it with kindness."

"Would that I could do more..." she murmured.

Catriona scowled but before she could ask what she meant, Logan approached and bowed.

"Forgive the interruption, my ladies. I must speak with ye Lady Lorna."

Lorna skipped her gaze from Catriona to Logan, and nodded slowly. Logan's sudden formality made Catriona deepen her scowl.

"As ye will. Pray excuse me. Have that missive to me by midday and I shall send my fastest rider," Lorna told her.

"Aye, thank ye."

Logan and Lorna left the hall and as Catriona turned, a chest blocked her way. She lifted her gaze to those stone cold eyes and grim lips.

"My lady," Gillean said softly.

"Aye?"

"Ye look very fine in that gown. The red compliments yer skin to perfection. I look forward to the day I can dress ye in only the best gowns..."

"My laird?"

"But yer lacing is a little bit loose. I shouldnae like my wife to be so... on display."

Gulping, her pulse beat heavily as he bore down on her. His hands came to her shoulders and he rotated her so her back was to him. She flinched when fingers brushed aside her hair but her limbs would not move nor would words of protest reach her lips. Laird Gillean dissolved her courage. Tears of frustration burned.

His fingers were cold and bony. Not like Finn's. She stiffened, hiding the shudder that racked her. This man might be her husband soon. If she couldn't stand his touch now, how would she survive the marriage bed?

Catriona closed her eyes as servants bustled around

them, folding away the tables and sweeping the floor—oblivious to her distress. Gillean tugged the laces, pulling the breath from her and taking an eternity to finish. She opened her eyes when she felt him tying the final bow and her gaze landed on Finn, silhouetted in the doorway. He seemed to occupy all of it. Pain radiated from him. Brow creased, he stared at her for too long—made her breaths grow short. Then, with a marginal shake of his head, he swivelled away and stormed into the bailey. She imagined his heavy footsteps kicking up dirt as he stomped away.

She hardly noticed when Gillean turned her around, a smug smile stretching the confines of his beard. "There. Perfect." His gaze crawled over her.

A tremble threatened to break free but she held herself stiff and thanked him distractedly. Why did Finn look so tortured? Did his heart ache like hers? Sometimes she thought she had him figured out and other days... was it more than lust? The full, painful sensation in her heart told her it was. At least for her.

***

Once again, wine beckoned him but he managed to stave off the hunger. He smirked as he stomped across the curtain wall, the night air ruffling his shirt, filling his lungs. Katelyn's scolding lingered in his mind. *Ye've been drinking.* He recalled her pretty nose, wrinkled in distaste. Instead he worked off energy stalking along the walls and around the bailey looking—nay, hoping—for some trouble. Anything to distract him from the memory of Gillean's hands upon Katelyn. The possessive look, the way he whispered in her ear. The longing in Katelyn's gaze. For him? He could only hope.

Could he? Her scent remained with him, even after he'd washed, marking him. Like a brand. Even the knowledge of her impending marriage did nothing to cool his need for her. He shouldn't be yearning for her. Shouldn't be hoping she wanted more. If he were a better man, he'd wish her well and pray for her happiness, but he was not. Selfishly, he wanted her. More than mead or wine, he wanted to take her and brand her as she had him. Stamp himself on her soul.

Like many a night, he found himself gazing up at her window. Warmth radiated from it. She would be in a chemise, the thin material moulding to her breasts. Unbound hair likely spiralled over her shoulders. Mayhap she had washed and her skin remained dewy and ebony curls clung to her face. A shudder swept through him and his blood boiled. He gripped the pommel of his sword. *Lord, give me strength.*

A movement sent his heart into his throat. His jaw dropped as Katelyn leaned out of the window. Sure enough, white cotton hugged her arms and her hair hung loose. Candlelight surrounded her in a fuzzy halo like an angel. She gazed out into the night, entrancing him. How he longed to know what she was thinking.

Did she think of him?

Her gaze snapped down, locking onto him. He peered around, realising the torchlight on the walls revealed him. Breath imprisoned in his throat, he met her challenge. Stance strong, chin lifted, he stared her out, waiting for her to crumble and retreat. The air around him became cloying and thick while his pulse pounded sickeningly. His arousal grew painful.

Abruptly, she turned away, broke the connection and left him panting and weak. He dropped his shoulders. Damnation. A moment to relieve himself was called for. Should he return to his chambers or just suffer it, like some kind of penance for a desire he should not have?

Swivelling, he stomped down the steps into the courtyard. He paused and gritted his teeth. Time alone would not cure him of her. And wine held no appeal any longer. He was lost.

The hall doors opened and a figure came barrelling out. He nearly cursed aloud when he realised it was Katelyn. Her chemise flowed around her legs, barely covered by a thin robe. He noted her bare feet and cursed properly this time. What was the lass doing outside in such a state?

Before he managed to ask her as much, she flung her arms around him and flattened a desperate kiss to his lips. He caught on quickly. With a growl, he bundled her to him, shaking hands splayed over her back and in her hair.

"Hell fire, Katie," he murmured as he took another kiss from her. Breaking away, he glanced around and shook his head. "What are ye doing? Anyone could see. Gillean could see."

"I care not," she whispered.

When she leaned up for a kiss, he released her, snatched an arm and dragged her over to the stables. One more frantic glance around and he shoved her into the doorway and pressed her against the wall. No candlelight greeted them here, only the glow from the torches outside permeated the building, slipping through the gaps between the wood. It was enough. He saw all he needed. Once more he speared his fingers under her hair, unable to resist those glossy lips, slick from his kisses. Katelyn whimpered when he captured her mouth and curled her fingernails into his back.

"Ye play a dangerous game, lass," he muttered against her mouth.

She tugged against the hold he had on her hair and eyed him. "I am no' afeared of Gillean."

"Ye are, ye cannae lie to me. But I mean with me. Ye play with fire here."

"I need ye, Finn. I am no' afeared of ye either. I'm willing to risk getting burned."

"Ach, we shall both be burned. No good shall come of

this."

His chest heaved at the enormity of it all, at what she said. He'd always known he was secretly weak. His bold endeavours and brash behaviour covered his fears. When others saw a warrior, Katelyn saw him for who he was. Weak for her.

And it didn't matter. Not here, not now. Not as long as he had her in his arms.

She flattened a kiss to the exposed skin at the opening of his shirt. He tilted his head back and pulled in a breath through his teeth.

"I cannae continue on not knowing," she told him, bringing up a finger to trace circles over the skin she'd just kissed as she rested her cheek against his chest. "I need to know, Finn. I have lived my whole life for others. This night I want to live for myself."

Thumbs pressed into her cheeks, he lifted her face up and searched her gaze. Had there been doubt or fear, he might have been able to turn her away but only bright need shone from her emerald eyes.

"Aye," he agreed and unbuckled the belt that held his sword, casting the leather and steel aside. "Tonight is for ye."

Then he pinned her with his chest against the wall and took her mouth. She was all scrabbling hands and rocking hips. Breathy sighs and feminine moans. He savoured and lapped at her, driven only by the need to bring her pleasure. Thoughts of anything apart from her shapely body and smooth skin drifted away like smoke in the wind. She tasted so damn divine. It forced a note from his throat that sounded vaguely animalistic.

He thrust against her to ease his need but it worsened. A hand to her rear, he clenched and moulded the soft flesh as she nipped his bottom lip and kissed down the side of his neck. Tingles traversed him, made his muscles tense.

Releasing her hair, he used his other hand to hitch up her chemise and robe. Underneath, warm, delicate skin awaited and he gripped her thigh, then moved up until he clasped her bottom. In one movement, he lifted her and she immediately latched her legs around his hips. Her juncture against his arousal was enough to send his eyes rolling into the back of his head.

"By God," he forced through a parched throat. He found the arch of her neck with his lips and her fingernails dug into his scalp as he frantically kissed every sweetly fragranced part from her shoulder to her ear. He paused to nip at her lobe, whispering, "For ye, wee lass. All for ye."

"Aye, oh aye," she said breathily.

Finn thrust against her—too hard probably—but he had little control over his movements. Her sounds and reactions drove him forward—*drove him mad.* This little vixen might have been a maiden, but she knew well how her body worked, and how to bring him to the edge.

She slipped a little and he lifted her again, slotting her perfectly against him. He stumbled away from the wall when she tilted herself to kiss him deeply, hands wound tightly in his hair. Arms wrapped about her, Finn manoeuvred them into an empty stall and pushed her up against the wall. Katelyn gasped when her back met the wall. Had he been too rough? But her desperate kisses across his face in search of his mouth soothed away his concern.

He lifted her higher until her breasts lined up with his face and he took a stiff peak straight into his mouth, sucking it through the cotton. She cried out and moved both hands to grip his shoulders. He nipped lightly with his teeth, relished the evidence of her desire, before nuzzling his way across to the other breast and paying it the same attention. The loose neckline of her chemise allowed him access to the rise of one breast and he kissed and sucked the supple flesh but it wasn't enough.

Hands supporting her, he carried her over to a hay bale. He smirked. Fate was mocking him, bringing him back here. But this time he'd have true satisfaction. He placed her on the bale and settled between her legs. His hands were shaky as he yanked at the neckline of her shift. Finally one rounded breast was revealed and he groaned. When he took it in his mouth with no barrier between them, Katelyn cried out his name.

He shushed her and blew across the taut peak, making

her renew her rocking motion. She tried to reach down to cup him but he brushed her hand away.

"For ye," he reminded her, licking his way between her breasts up to her collarbone. "And I'll no' last if ye touch me, Katie. Yer too much for a man to take."

"I want to touch ye," she complained while he kissed up the side of her neck.

"Soon," he assured her. His gut fisted when he realised that wasn't true. He had her for one night, nothing more. The tightening eased when he brought a hand up between them and cupped a breast. He might regret not being able to do more, but he would not let fear ruin this.

He drew away to look at her. Delicate pale skin, trembling breasts, thighs parted. God almighty, not even a saint could resist. He lunged forward and she nearly toppled off the bale, so desperate was his kiss. He managed to slip her robe from her shoulders and find the hem of her chemise while she tangled her tongue furiously with his.

Breaking away for the merest moment, he removed the shift and flung it aside. Katelyn's hand worked feverishly at the pin of his plaid. Still they kissed as he helped her with the rest of his garments. As soon as he was undressed, he kneeled between her thighs and flattened her against him.

"Are ye cold?" he asked between kisses.

"Nay."

Finn smoothed his hands up and down her back, taking pleasure in the softness. He found the dip of her bottom and traced it with his fingers, then sketched a path up her spine. She trembled in his arms and arched her hips. Damp heat made his head swim and he cursed roughly. He wished to God he could be more careful, treat her like a queen, but his need was too great. His touches were rough and fraught but Katelyn met him, touch for touch. Her soft fingers were as eager. She tugged his braid, dug her nails into him, even nipped his shoulder with her teeth. He'd truly met his match in Katelyn.

Sliding a hand between them, he found her sex and she jerked when he circled her nub. All that obvious desire for him made him impossibly hard. He toyed there for as long as he was able, his body taut with restraint. Finn sank a finger into her and she went rigid. Then she urged him deeper and he followed it with another finger. Soon she rode his digits, head thrown back, hair cascading and brushing against the arm he used to support her. His nostrils flared, his skin heated. Torture and ecstasy in one. A sight he'd never forget.

"Now," she said so quietly, he barely heard her. "Now," she repeated forcefully.

Nodding—not trusting himself with words—he withdrew his fingers and spread out her discarded robe over the bale. He urged her down until she lay across it and settled himself between her thighs again.

Her gaze raked over him and the glint in her eyes told him she liked what she saw. He was so hard and ready for her. Her sex touched his aching shaft and they both groaned aloud.

The sensation sparked a frenzy in them, one that would only be quenched by lovemaking. Finn moved his hands to her hair, across her breasts and under her rear, moulding her to him as he stared down at her. Never had a moment been more intimate. But he couldn't take the time to treasure it. His need for this magical woman was too great. He kissed her mouth, neck, collarbone and she wriggled against him, spreading her lips over whatever flesh she could find. Her soft lips dancing across his skin increased the throb in his body and before realising what he'd done, he found her hips again and he joined them in one short, sharp thrust.

She cried out, and he froze.

"Damnation."

He tried to pull away but she held him there. By God, why couldn't he have been more careful? He'd just taken her innocence like some barbarian. Somehow he remained still, his arms trembling as he held himself above her. The tight heat forced sweat to prick on his forehead. She gazed boldly up at him, as if absorbing the new sensation. The tiniest movement of her hips and her body relaxing had him making a sound in the back of his throat and he lowered himself, weight held one arm, his other hand stroking her hair.

They kissed unsteadily, picking up speed until they ravaged each other's mouths. Finn knew Katelyn was passionate, but her reaction staggered him. He'd wager no man realised such an astounding woman lay behind her fragile, beautiful features. Mayhap he was the only man to unlock this side of her.

Finn moved erratically, with little finesse, but it seemed he could do no wrong. Her body fluttered in response. The primal rhythm overtook him, only her scent and her hot staggered breaths registered. The taste and feel of her filled his senses. Scalding gratification began to burn through his body so he slid a hand between them and rotated a finger against her folds. Her mouth slipped from his and her body tensed.

"Oh, Finn," she cried. "Sweet Mary…."

He saw it unfold. Through the fog of his own pleasure he didn't see it as clearly as he'd have liked but he still observed the widening of her eyes when she peaked, body shaking and bucking. Finn tucked her head into the crook of his neck, still relentlessly driving into her. She would never forget this—never forget *him*.

This was it for him, he realised, as the sensations boiled inside him. While the lovemaking was unlike anything he'd ever felt, it was the feeling in his chest, his feelings for this woman that made it so much more.

She continued to buck into his lunges, in spite of

her exhausted state, and he helped her, using her body to bring himself to the edge and over. He spilled inside her, the fiercest release of his life.

"Finn," she breathed in his ear, the sound wrapping around his heart.

He sagged against her, despair replacing satisfaction. What had he done?

CHAPTER EIGHT

Catriona winced and tried to rub her face. It itched. But her arms were trapped. *Trapped.*

Her chest compressed and she twisted frantically. A male grumble pulled her out of her panic and she froze.

Finn.

She squeezed her eyes shut and opened them again, forcing away the sleep in her eyes. The light of dawn streamed in through the gaps in the wood and the open front of the stables. Straw prickled her skin. One strong arm and leg enveloped her, pinned her down. Her robe tangled around Finn's legs, the green silk somehow looking impeccable against his sun kissed skin. Catriona put a hand to his shoulder and relished his warm, taut skin. Scars marred his back, some barely visible and others streaking across his perfect skin like lightning bolts—proof of his bold nature. Odd how he cared so little for his own welfare. She traced the line of muscle in his arm, marvelling at how he'd withheld that strength with her. There were moments when he'd been rough, but she trusted him to know what she needed.

Considering her body, she conceded she was paying the price now. She winced as she shifted her legs. Losing her maidenhood was never going to be pleasant, but she'd hadn't expected such an experience. Or had she? Why else would she have given herself to him? Finn had been so considerate, in spite of his—*their*—desperate need for one another. Her heart dropped. How she longed to find out more. Any other lover would never match up to Finn.

She laughed at herself. As if she could ever have another lover after this. When her father came for her, she anticipated hiding away. Without Finn, who knew how her fears might manifest themselves? It was unlikely any other man would be as understanding of her nightmares.

Scuffing footsteps outside sent her heart rebounding against her ribs.

"Finn!" She shook his arm.

He grumbled again, lifted his head and gave her a sleepy smile that melted her insides. His hair fell across his face, mussed and scattered with straw. He eyed her from under his brow, lines creasing it as he took in her naked state. His smile tilted.

"Finn, 'tis dawn."

He blinked, glanced around and scrabbled to standing. "Damnation."

Together they hunted down their clothes and dressed. He helped her shrug into her robe as she battled with the pin for his plaid.

"I dinnae know how I'm going to explain this." She motioned up and down her.

He peered around the doorway. "Fear not. The sun is only just up. Most of the household is still abed."

"We should not have taken such a risk. What if Gillean sees me?"

His jaw clenched, his eyes hardened. "Aye, of course. Gillean. Ye wouldnae want yer future husband to know of yer nocturnal activities."

Pain stabbed her heart and she pressed her lips together. Brushing the straw from her robe and plucking some out of her hair, she gathered her breath. Why did he have to make it sound so sordid? Had he not wanted her just as badly? She hadn't intended for Finn to make love to her but she had been so consumed by him, she had to see him. And, as usual, once in his presence all sense deserted her.

But it had taken two. And now he behaved as if she'd instigated it all. Talking about her as if she was some kind of...

"Dinnae speak as if I am a whore," she said quietly.

"This was a mistake," he bit out.

The agony in her chest expanded and made her limbs shake. She ran her fingers through her hair and lifted her chin. "That much I know. But I didnae expect ye to talk so to me."

He paused, skimmed his gaze over her and shook his head. Clearly he regretted getting close to her. Did he feel he'd betrayed the memory of his wife? Was it something else? Mayhap he had only wanted a quick tumble and feared she'd fallen for him. Well, she would have to set him straight. She'd known all along their attraction was doomed.

"Help me to my chambers unseen and we shall speak no more of this. Ye can forget it ever happened."

A muscle twitched in his jaw and he jerked slightly, as if she'd struck out at him. Finally, he nodded. "Aye, 'twould be best. Soon ye shall be married."

Why did he repeat that all the time? It was not as if she did not know. She only hoped it would not come to pass. It had been a foolish move, making love to Finn. Gillean would question why she was no longer a maiden if it ever came to that. Her stomach churned and she cast her gaze up, praying that did not lie in her future.

"Just return me to the keep," she whispered, coming to his side as he put his head around the doorway. For once, she needed the refuge of her chambers. She needed to wash away his scent, his touch, and straighten her confused thoughts.

And she must come up with a way to deal with Gillean.

Finn had proved such a distraction she kept forgetting what was at stake. The safety of Bute. Gillean had to be appeased if her father still did not have the king's support. Until she knew otherwise, she had to continue her ruse.

Fingers pressed to her lips, she shook her head. What had she been thinking? She'd given herself to a man who didn't even know who she was.

"Come then." Finn did not wait for a response. He snatched her hand and led her across the bailey.

She scanned the empty courtyard with a sigh of relief. A few men were high up on the walls but their backs were to them as they surveyed the land for danger. They hurried across the dry mud, hand in hand. If only his touch did not make her feel so safe. Indeed, Finn had to be the most dangerous man of all. If he had not already broken her heart, leaving him would surely finish the job.

He led her up the few stone steps to the hall door and pushed it open slightly. Finn put his face to the gap and Catriona peered around wildly, her heart thudding. Anyone could come along and discover them. What would they think if they saw her in her chemise, hand in hand with Finn? They would think they had taken a tumble.

She almost laughed. They'd be right about that. For Finn, it had certainly been a mere tumble. And for her? It was lovemaking. Without a doubt.

The door squeaked when Finn pushed it further open. Catriona grimaced, ready for someone to pounce on them and demand to know what they had done, but no one came. A servant scurried about at the end of the hall, laying the top table, but he paid them no heed. Mayhap he would gossip about them later but as long as Gillean or Lorna did not see them, servant's talk meant little.

Finn urged her across the hall and up the stairs to the gallery. Still clasping her hand, he led her to her chamber. Just as he put a hand to the door handle, footsteps made her lift her head. Finn dropped her hand and took a step back as Gillean strode along the balcony from his chambers.

"Lady Katelyn," he greeted, fastening his hands behind and studying her. "What are ye doing out of yer chambers dressed in so little?"

Gillean's eyes narrowed and he licked his lips. He dropped his gaze to her breasts and she clamped her robe around her, sure he had seen her nipples dark against the linen. The thought twisted her stomach.

"I-I..."

"Lady Katelyn thought she heard a noise and was looking for aid. I happened to already be awake," Finn interjected smoothly.

"Really?" Gillean mused and brought a hand up to stroke his beard. "How fortunate for ye, my lady, that Finn should be awake at this early hour."

She smiled tightly. "Indeed. But it seems I was mistaken. All is well."

"That is good news indeed." Gillean's expression lightened and he smiled. "I hope ye are well rested. We have the wedding plans to finalise this day."

"Aye, my laird. I hope we shall have word from my father soon, so that he may join us."

"We can but hope, but I must return to my lands soon," he warned before sending an indulgent smile to Finn. "These women are sentimental creatures. Ye have done well not to have married again."

Finn nodded, his expression tight. Katelyn noticed he had curled both fists at his side.

"Of course, they forget that marriage is a business transaction for men," Gillean continued. "But I have done well to secure such a prize, do ye no' think Finn?"

Surely he saw Finn's tense stance? Did Gillean intend to rile him? What did he want? Mayhap he suspected there was more to their presence on the gallery than they'd said. The laird was certainly a shrewd man. But if he anticipated sparking a reaction from Finn, he'd have little chance. Even her making love to him had not breached his barriers.

Catriona fought the temptation to protest such a description but the fight had left her, sapped by Finn's dismissal.

Finn squared his shoulders. "I would know naught of prizes, Gillean, but ye have yerself a fine woman. Now, if ye'll excuse me, I have much to see to." He bowed to Katelyn. "Good day, my lady."

She did not respond—did not trust herself to. He stormed down the stairs, running a hand through his dishevelled hair as he went. The memory of how his fair hair had felt under her fingers made them tingle. The desire to curl up and shut away the world grew stronger but she kept her spine straight and met Gillean's perceptive gaze.

"I should dress."

"Ye should, my lady. Ye shouldnae be out of yer chambers dressed so." She caught the reprimand in his tone. "No matter how enticing ye might look."

Catriona gripped her silk robe until her fingers grew tingly.

"I have high hopes the priest shall arrive this day," he informed her.

"That... that is good news."

"It is." His voice dropped. "Then I shall be able to enjoy such a sight every morn."

Eyes wide, Catriona fell against her door. The lascivious shade to his expression made his already cold eyes, darker, more dangerous. She gulped and fumbled for the door handle.

"I... I... good day, my laird." She twisted the handle and slipped into her chamber, slamming the door shut and leaning against it. A chuckle resonated through the wood. She cringed.

Did he know? Lord, what had she done? It would be well enough if it was only her future on the line but she held the fate of her friends and father in her hands. Appeasing Laird Gillean and finding a way to delay the wedding until the messenger reached Bute had to be her priority—*not* Finn. She slapped her hands to her hot cheeks. What had she done?

***

He danced back away from the blade as it swept close to his neck. Too close. Logan was a strong fighter but Finn was off his game. His body ached from sleeping in the straw and images of Katelyn played through his mind.

He'd behaved a fool.

Finn swung in retaliation and their blades crashed together sending shudders up his arm. Dust from the mud of the bailey kicked up around them. When he might have been able to take a second slice at Logan, he missed his chance by being too slow and Logan came at him again, pushing his blade to the ground.

No other man practiced, only them. Boots scraping the dirt and his pounding heart throbbed in his ears. Jumping back, Finn lunged once more only for Logan to sidestep him, grab his pommel and draw him close enough to nearly run him through. The two men faced one another, heavy breaths blowing between them.

"Something is amiss, Finn," Logan declared as he released Finn's sword and pushed him back lightly.

Finn swiped the arm of his shirt across his damp brow. "Naught is amiss."

Logan shook his head and slipped his sword into his belt. "Finn, ye are one of the finest swordsmen I know. For yer years of training I cannae compete, yet I beat ye easily this day."

"Yer a fine swordsman."

"I learned swordsmanship the hard way, as ye well know. I have none of yer finer skills." Logan slapped a hand to Finn's arm. "Anyhow, dinnae change the subject. What plagues ye?"

A smile teased Finn's lips, begged to be released, but instead he sighed. How was it Katelyn forced all his defences down?

"Is it Katelyn?"

"'Tis naught, Logan."

"Naught doesnae throw ye off yer game like that. In all the years we've know each other, I've never seen ye this consumed by a lass."

"Consumed?" Finn's brows darted up. Logan had already inferred he recognised Finn's need for Katelyn but he thought he'd thrown him off the scent with his flippant remarks.

"Aye, consumed. 'Tis hard to miss the way ye watch her, Finn. And the way she looks at ye."

Finn kicked a stone and strolled away to settle on the wall. If Logan saw it, did Gillean? And the way Katelyn looked at him? Earlier, all he'd seen was hurt and disgust. He'd practically called her a whore. Shame heated his face. He'd taken something precious and thrown it away. What had happened between them had been more than a mere tumble.

"It doesnae matter," Finn grumbled. "She shall be married soon enough."

"There is always a way, old friend. Ye would do well to take a chance."

Finn let slip a depreciative laugh as Logan rested next to him. "A chance on what? I took chances once before and I lost everything, Logan. I'll no' do that again. She will marry Gillean and I shall return home and there ends our story. Anyway, what of ye? I dinnae see ye married to my sister."

Logan bristled. "Yer sister willnae have me. Alas I am still a mere peasant boy in her eyes and I fear I always will be."

"But…" Finn fought down the brotherly protectiveness, recalling Logan's words of love, "she let ye into her bed, did she not?"

"Aye, and declared it a mistake."

Pinching the bridge of his nose, Finn nodded. Hadn't he done the same to Katelyn? And while she reacted with cold dignity, he'd been aware it was his angry reaction that prompted such behaviour. But the mere mention of Gillean and her marriage sent a surge of jealousy rolling through him that clouded any judgement.

"My sister cares for ye and I doubt she thinks ye as a peasant boy," he finally declared. "She is always quick to come to yer defence."

"Well, I shallnae give up and I dinnae think ye should, Finn. Ye must surely know the lass is worth the heartache." He came to his feet and patted him on the shoulder. "I have duties to see to. I'll bid ye good day."

"Aye, and to ye, Logan." Finn dropped his head and considered Logan's words as the man strolled off.

Worth the heartache? Mayhap. But it was not his decision. Katelyn was contracted to marry Gillean. What else could he do? He'd ruined her with his selfishness. It mattered little how she felt about him. He lifted his head. However, his words to her earlier still vexed him. He would have to apologise for them. How could he let her believe he thought her a whore?

Unfortunately there was little he could do to make up for his taking her innocence. Not even the most heartfelt apology would repair that damage. Damnation. His gut clenched as if he'd been punched. He had even spilled inside her. He dropped his face into his hands. What if he'd not only taken her maidenhood but planted his child inside her?

***

Catriona wouldn't have heard the soft tap at her door had she been asleep but in spite of being tired, sleep refused to come. Her mind was a whirl of panic and plans. The priest looked to be arriving on the morrow according to the missive they'd received that day. Throwing back the covers, she padded over to the door and drew it open. Would it be Gillean? He'd been so bold with his attentions, she wouldn't have been surprised.

She peered out the gap and sucked in a startled breath. He'd seemed so angry, regretful. Why was he here now? She almost shut the door in his face. How could she face him now? Her cheeks burned at the memory of her wanton behaviour.

"Katie," he said sorrowfully.

It stabbed her wounded heart. She wanted to hear her real name on his lips. "What do ye want, Finn?"

"Let me in," he demanded softly.

With a sigh, she stepped back, allowing him to push open the door and enter the room. He seemed to take up all the space in her chambers. Candlelight gilded his hair, highlighted the dark circles under his eyes and the grooves in his brow. His brows knitted as he studied her, as if he were in pain.

Catriona clamped her arms around herself and held on

tightly. Even now, she wanted him. While her heart ached and her stomach cramped, she needed him. Her body betrayed her.

Her heart betrayed her.

She loved a man who didn't even know who she truly was. Who could never really love her as she loved him. He was still wrapped up in his dead wife and child, any fool could see that, and who would blame him. That he cared so deeply for them only made her love him more.

"Are ye well?"

She blinked up at him. "Aye, I am well," she replied stiffly.

He stared at his feet then lifted his gaze to her. "I didnae mean...."

"I know well ye didnae mean to take a tumble with me, Finn. Ye made that clear."

"Nay, I meant... I didnae mean to hurt ye. Physically or...."

He looked so lost, her heart almost burst for him. "Emotionally?"

"Aye."

"Fear not, I shall recover I am sure."

Finn scuffed a foot across the floorboard. "Also, I wanted to check... I mean I shouldnae have... if ye should carry my child, I should like to know."

She closed her eyes briefly and put a hand against the post of the bed for support. Lord, she hadn't even considered that. She could take some tea which would help prevent babes but with everything going on, she had forgotten. What if it was too late?

"I am sure naught will happen. 'Twas only once after all," she replied blithely.

"I should still like to know." He took a step forward and she shrank back. "What shall ye do if ye conceive my child? Will ye pretend it is Gillean's?"

This thought appeared to pain him and his brow furrowed further. She itched to smooth away his concern. It was for nothing, after all. If her father didn't turn up on the morrow, she'd have to marry Gillean and pray her father rescued her before the laird found out the truth. After all, Gillean could not hold her to a contract that did not have her name on it.

She shuddered as she considered what she might have to suffer to keep up the pretence.

Finn touched her cheek. "Forgive me, I didnae mean to scare ye."

"Ye didnae scare me."

"Forgive my behaviour then." He dipped his head and wrapped a curl of hair around one finger, staring at it as he stroked its length.

"There is naught to forgive." Her legs trembled when she saw the darkening in his eyes. His gaze dropped to her lips, then to her breasts—her nipples likely stood out against the white of her chemise—and back up to meet her gaze.

"There is. I took advantage of ye. I behaved like a boar."

"Ye didnae take advantage, Finn. I gave myself willingly."

"And I shouldnae have taken it. I thought myself a better man than that but I was wrong."

Catriona shook her head slowly. He meant to torture himself and she refused to allow that. He might have hurt her but she had no wish for him to hurt any more than necessary. The man already carried too much around on those great shoulders.

"Ye are a good man, Finn. Dinnae say otherwise."

"Not good enough for ye." He smirked. "Forgive me, I shouldnae have spoken so."

She searched his gaze. What did he mean? A spark of hope lit in her chest but she tamped it down. Even if he felt as she did, there could be no future for them. On the morrow—if she could not delay the wedding any longer—she would be wed to Gillean.

"*Ye* are too good for me," she said gently, giving in and pressing away the dips etched into his forehead. "Ye have been kind and patient." She cupped his cheek and he leaned into her hand with a tiny groan of surrender.

"What am I to do with ye, Katie? I am a weak man around ye." He put his arms around her, placed his hands against her lower back and pulled her into him. "Ye are to be married…" he murmured as he urged her down against the bed.

She nodded, warm gratification flowing through her at the feel of his hard body against hers.

"On the morrow ye shall be another's." He laid his lips to her neck.

"Aye," she whispered.

"I can offer ye naught."

"Aye, I know."

"I cannae resist ye."

"I know," she repeated. "And I."

"Just one more night," he breathed into her ear.

"Aye, one more night."

One last chance to feel loved and treasured for the first time in her life, even if it wasn't true. He felt something for her—whether it was love, she knew not—but the way Finn touched her and worshipped her body was enough. He was no man of great words but he said much with his fingers. Everything was unravelling. Soon, something would change. If she couldn't persuade Gillean to delay the wedding further she'd be married. And if her father ever came to her rescue, her real identity would come out and she'd return to Bute.

Still, before long he would forget her and her deception.

Finn had offered her no commitments, no words of love, and she doubted he ever intended to.

But for now she wanted one more night. Another memory

to carry her through whatever the next few days brought. Catriona parted her lips in invitation and he hovered over her.

"No' so hasty this time, wee lass." He skimmed a finger over her lips, down her throat and circled it lightly. "So fragile," he murmured. "Yer skin is so pale and beautiful. I shallnae touch it again after this night."

She nodded numbly. Against the painful throb of her heart, warmth flowed through her at his touch, the combination confusing and exhilarating, as if his seductions might soothe away some of the agony.

"I shallnae kiss ye again," he whispered.

He tucked his arm further under her back and held her close before lowering his lips to hers. The instant bolt of awareness that jolted through her still surprised her. He shoved her chemise from her shoulder. Dragging his mouth away from hers, he bit down on her bare skin and she moaned. He used his teeth to rake across her skin to her neck and took a moment to suck and lick there. Katelyn writhed under his weight

He fumbled with the laces at the front of her shift, trying to part the material but his hands seemed uncontrollable. With a growl, he gave up his fight with the laces and rolled so she landed on top of him. Her legs came to either side of his hips and his hardness pressed against her sex. She rocked against him and plunged her hands into his hair to kiss him fiercely.

Tongues tangling, barely time to take a breath, Finn grasped her hips and she moved eagerly as flickers of gratification already pulsed through her.

Her hair trailed over him, like a curtain, hiding them from the world. The candlelight slid over his features, flickering and dancing. Catriona stroked her hands over his stubbled jaw and touched the scar on his lip, twisted the small braid in his hair. His hands found the neckline of her chemise once more and he tugged forcefully. She ran her palms up and down his chest, urging him on, and his plaid loosened and fell to his side. Her nails hit his stomach, pressing under his shirt and he hissed.

Catriona gasped when his desperate tugs rent her chemise nearly in two so the curves of her breasts were visible to his eager gaze

"By God, Katie, ye are more perfect than I ever dreamed," he murmured in awe.

She lifted her breasts, entreating him to touch them while the soft flesh vibrated gently with her wanting breaths. The rosy tips tightened under his scrutiny.

A smile crept across her face. "Ye dreamed of me?"

"Aye. Many a night."

"I dreamed of ye too," she admitted.

"Come here, my sweet lassie." He used his hands to coax her forward, bringing her breasts to his mouth.

Finn sucked on one breast while he palmed the other,

always avoiding her tight nipples. She groaned in frustration. His hips thrust up, mimicking what she longed for him to do but he appeared determined to slow things down. He moved his attention to her other breast, holding her against him now with both hands. She skimmed her hands down his sides, treasuring the flex of his muscles and waiting for that hot mouth on her aching tips. Whatever he felt for her at least she knew he desired her just as much. Rising, she tugged his shirt up and he helped her pull his garments off. His hair rumpled, his eyes softened. Catriona trailed a finger over the dips of his stomach and over the fine golden hair leading down.

"Yer so beautiful," she murmured and he chuckled. "What? Ye dinnae think a man can be beautiful?"

He lifted those great shoulders, amusement in his gaze. "Lasses are beautiful. *Ye* are beautiful. Yer made so perfectly." Finn ran his fingers up her sides, tracing her curves.

She smiled. "As are ye, Finn."

Fingers flexing around his arousal, she trailed her hair over him, watched the undulation of his muscles as his breaths rasped, and licked the tip. He bucked his hips.

"By God, Katie," he spluttered when she took him further into her mouth.

The taste and texture of him danced on her tongue. She'd heard of such a way of pleasuring a man but she did not know it could bring her pleasure too. Her body pulsed as rough fingers winnowed through her hair. Catriona took him deeper and he throbbed against her tongue. She worked up and down him, hand clasped around the base. His scent filled her nostrils, musky and masculine.

"Enough now," he ordered, gripping her arms to pull her up. She straightened and licked her lips—savoured the taste of him. "Katie, yer enough to send a man out of his wits."

Knowing fingers sought out her heat, rubbing and coaxing pleasure from her. She pitched against him and traced his features and body with her gaze. Never again would she have this—*have him*, she reminded herself. She had to imprint him in her memory. Finn—naked and full of desire for her. It filled her with power and strength. If she was to get through the next few seasons, she would need that strength.

"Finn," she moaned. "Finn, I need ye. Dinnae make me wait."

"Ach, ye know I cannae deny ye."

He grasped her hips and drove up into her. Her cry split the air. His heat speared her, shocking and soothing at the same time. Calming her need, yet igniting a new one. Finn helped her into a rhythm and warmth coiled in her belly. He stared up at her. How she wished she knew what he was thinking. Gazing into his eyes, she could almost believe he loved her. With one look, he made her feel impossibly beautiful and amazing.

Sensation built like a growing flame. Her breaths laboured as she rode him and her skin grew slick. Perspiration shimmered on Finn's torso. Catriona scraped her fingernails down him and he groaned.

Never again.

Never again would she have him like this. She wouldn't feel his touch or hear his laugh. See his smile or blush under his attention. An ache gathered in her throat. Her vision became cloudy. Before she realised what had happened, tears rolled down her cheeks onto his chest.

"Katie?"

Suddenly, she was lifted from him and placed onto the bed. He leaned over her, a hand pushing away the tears from her cheek. Catriona gripped his arm and fought to keep more tears at bay. This rough warrior could never know how much his actions meant to her. Without him, the past few sennights would have been torture. He gave so much but thought so little of himself. Why could he not see he deserved another chance at happiness? Finn was *meant* to have a woman to love.

Just not her.

Eyes squeezed shut, more tears threatened to come. She pictured a future with Finn. A life filled with love and several fair haired children. If things were different—if she wasn't lying or committed to another—would that ever have happened or would he stay forever locked behind his wall of grief?

"Katie, look at me." He continued to smooth his callused hands over her cheek. "Why do ye cry?"

Catriona opened her eyes and gave him a weak smile. "'Tis naught."

"I dinnae wish to make ye cry."

She shook her head. "'Tis nae ye."

His expression grew grim. "'Tis Gillean?"

"In a way."

Finn paused, his hand stilling on her cheek. She searched his gaze for an answer but none came that made any sense. Deep burning love reflected in those eyes but mayhap that was only hers. Her chest clogged with emotion again, until it became unbearable.

"Dinnae speak on it anymore. Only love me, Finn."

He nodded, throat bobbing. "Aye, that I can do."

He coaxed her onto her side and tucked her into the crook of his legs. He palmed a breast and she released a breath of gratification. His manhood pushed against her bottom and she wriggled as the desperate ache renewed. Scraping her hair aside, his lips met the sensitive skin of her neck and the top of her spine. Catriona leaned into his kisses while he rolled and plucked a nipple. After so long desiring his touch there, it electrified her. Skin tingled and moisture gathered.

"Love me, Finn," she begged, unsure whether she was

pleading for him to fill her or simply confess his feelings.

"I will," he whispered in her ear. "I will love ye until ye forget yer name. Until ye can think of no one but me. Ye shall remember this, Katie. Remember me. When all has changed around ye and time has passed, still ye shall think of when ye came apart in my arms."

Who knew if his words were meant to be comforting, but comfort her they did. He was right. She'd forever carry him in her heart and he would give her the strength she needed to protect her home and do her duty. His words were the closest thing to love she'd ever heard so she vowed to treasure them.

A hand slipped between her legs, parting her for him and he slid easily into her sheath, still slick with lust. He moved his hand to her hip and clasped it so he could glide into her with ease. Whispers slid over her skin—words of affection, how beautiful she was—as he took her higher and higher. Trembling and keening, she splintered apart, a slow, full release that brought fresh tears to her eyes.

Finn's harsh groan echoed in her ear as he gripped her tight and convulsed against her. The fingers on her hips dug in and relaxed suddenly. Warmth filled her and she sighed, limbs loosening against him. He wrapped his arms around her waist and she held them there, as if to keep him with her forever.

He kissed her ear. "Rest well, wee lass. I'll stay awhile but I shall be gone before dawn."

She swallowed the lump in her throat and held him tighter.

***

With the sun creeping up behind him, Finn urged Dìleas into a gallop. When they reached the brow of the hill, he pulled her to a stop and patted her flank. Gazing down at the keep, he found himself where Katelyn had been not so long ago. He'd thought he'd lost her that day. Ach, not that he ever had her.

Filling his lungs with air, he had Dìleas set off at a wild pace. He should have been satisfied, he thought. A night of hot lovemaking shouldn't have left him with energy burning under his skin, with a pang of hunger in his belly for more.

More Katelyn.

He had to leave. He would say his farewells to his sister and be gone this day. How could he watch Katelyn wed another? He'd been selfish enough bedding her again. Foolish enough too. Yet again, he'd spilled inside of her with no thought for her safety or future. He didn't even know how she would explain to Gillean how she had lost her maidenhood. Women were tricky, he knew that much, but not Katelyn. He had taken all she could give and thrown her to the wolves.

He was the worst kind of a man. He'd failed to protect Alice and the babe, and now he'd failed Katelyn. Still, she would move on, have babes and live well enough. He might not trust

Gillean but what could he do? He was no better for her and she was contracted to marry the man. How could he stomp in, demand Gillean relinquish her and destroy any chance of a good life for her? If he did not leave Kilcree that might be what he would do. He had to leave before he did anything even more foolish.

The breeze buffeted him, refreshing him but not removing the throb in his heart. He'd never forget her, to be sure. Had he ever met a woman so giving in bed? So divine, her fragile beauty only increased as he touched her, like a flower turning toward the sun. He smiled at the memory of those soft lips curving upward then touching him. Finn gripped the reins.

This would not do. If he wasn't careful he'd put himself deep in his cups again. Odd how one scolding remark had taken away any hunger for wine or ale though. Likely he would always recall her light admonishment and wrinkled nose.

He cast his gaze over the castle while he rode Dìleas down a steep embankment. The sun now sat just above it, as if balancing on the ramparts. The orange glow warmed the stone. His gaze travelled to Katelyn's window as it always did and he clenched the reins until they dug into his palm. He had to surmount this. Leaving was his only choice. Once he was back in his small cottage in Glencolum, the memories would fade. Her scent wouldn't be able to follow him across the hills; her laughter couldn't reach him there. She might invade his dreams sometimes though.

Nay, he'd remember her. He snorted. He'd wanted to brand himself in her memory for some sadistic reason. She'd as much as admitted she had no wish to marry Gillean. In some twisted way, he believed the memory of him—a selfish, cowardly man—would carry her through the misery of an arranged marriage. However, he thought it more likely she would forget him soon enough and he would be left with the lingering doubt.

Finn shook his head and eased the horse into a trot. Lorna needed to know he was leaving. He vowed to avoid Katelyn if he could. And then he would be gone and Katelyn would be married.

CHAPTER NINE

Gillean watched Catriona closely. All throughout the morning meal, she felt his gaze on her. She yawned. Hopefully she could retreat to her chambers before long. She simply had to avoid any more talk of the wedding. Her eyes itched from crying and her body ached—but in the most beautiful way. If only the ache in her chest was the same. True to his word, Finn had left by dawn. She hadn't seen him all morning and neither had Lorna. Had he truly gone without a word? She thought he'd meant he would leave her chambers but mayhap he meant to leave Kilcree too.

She fingered her gown as she waited for Lorna to finish speaking with Logan. They conferred by the fire pit, their words hushed but urgent. Whatever they were speaking of, she did not wish to interfere. Gillean lingered in the periphery of her vision, like a wolf eyeing his prey as he sat on a large carved chair, tucked into one corner. He had yet to say anything more than the basic greetings and that made her more nervous. Gone were the overly-friendly touches and the words that were intended to be charming. Coldness had crept over him. Here was the true Gillean, she concluded. The one she'd be marrying.

Logan swivelled on his heels and walked briskly out of the hall, a scowl on his face. Only the three of them now remained. The servants were busy in the kitchens or in the chambers making up the beds and the men-at-arms had taken up their positions while the night watchmen slept in the armoury. The silence made her clench her hands together.

Lorna shook her head and finally turned to face Catriona, a tight smile on her face. "Is all well?"

"Well enough. Is all well with ye, Lorna?" Catriona asked, noting the lines of tension around Lorna's usually youthful eyes.

"Aye, aye." She waved a hand. "Do ye need something? For the wedding mayhap?"

"Nay, I just wondered… I know it has no' been long, but have we word from the coast yet?"

Lorna gave her sympathetic smile. "Nay, and be assured, as soon as we have news from Bute, I shall pass it on to ye." She patted her hand "Ye must miss yer father very much. And yer sister… Catriona, is it?"

Catriona had to bite back the correction on her tongue. All her life she'd been correcting people when they thought her Katelyn. It was a wonder she hadn't slipped up already but she could not do so now, not when she was so near to the end.

Hopefully.

She shrugged. "I wasnae close to my family," Catriona confessed, "but I shouldnae wish them harm and I long for word of Bute. Besides," she flicked a peek at Gillean, "my father should want desperately to be here for my wedding."

"I understand. Alas, Gillean is an impatient man and may not wait much longer. He has many duties and must return home to see to them."

Catriona nodded. "Aye, I know." And it was going to be impossible to delay any longer. Her future hung on a precipice and she was losing the will to fight. Without Finn by her side her strength deserted her.

Lorna patted her hand again. "I must see to my ledgers but if ye need me, I shall be in my solar."

"Aye, thank ye." Catriona drew up her shoulders. Hadn't Finn, in his way, intended for her to stay strong. His words to her were meant to carry her through whatever was to come. She eyed Lorna's progress up the wooden stairs and debated speaking with Gillean. But his folded arms and frosty demeanour had her skirting around him and making for the stairs herself.

He stood suddenly and blocked her way. She glanced

around the empty hall, a chill sweeping through her as if a breeze had blown in.

"On the morrow, we shall be wed," he told her, expression stern. "The priest arrives this day. One more day is all ye shall have and no more."

"But, my laird—Gillean," she tried, softening her tone, "my father should be here soon. I know he would wish to witness the joining of our families. I ask but a few days of ye, 'tis all."

"Nay. No more delays. Ye dinnae behave like the excited bride-to-be. I was told ye were keen on our match and I am tired of yer behaviour. I should have myself a docile, obedient wife and I willnae be patient any longer. Ye have made a mockery out of me and I shallnae tolerate any more of this disobedience. Ye might no' be my wife yet but ye are my betrothed and I expect ye to behave as such." He glowered at her. "On the morrow, we wed."

She gulped. On the morrow? It was too soon. Her situation was hopeless but she had to try.

"Pray, my laird, I dinnae mean to disrespect ye. I am all excited anticipation for our wedding but ye must see that I need my father by my side before I take such a step."

"Nay, I dinnae see, and I dinnae see ye being obedient as I ask. Ye might be a bonny lass but that carries no weight with me. I shall put ye in yer place should I have to."

His face reddened and she backed away, eyes wide. What had she done? Now she had incensed him. His hand darted out and he snatched her arm, stopping her retreat. She gasped as fingers pinched her arm.

"My laird," she protested, tugging away. "My laird, pray there is no need—"

"There is," he hissed, spittle flying from his lips. "Ye are a little deceiving whore and I shall have it no longer. Ye shall be mine, body and soul on the morrow."

"Gillean—"

"No more lies, Catriona," he spat out.

"Pray, Gillean." She tugged away again but his grip tightened. Her strength deserted her as his words sank in. Catriona lifted her hand to her mouth. "Ye know?"

"Aye, I know." He reeled her in until he had hold of both her arms. "I know ye intended to trick me. I know yer sister—my true bride—is dead. I received word on my travels of her death. And," his lips turned up into a sneer, "of yer father's."

"My father's?"

"Aye, killed by a Norse arrow."

Her head swam and she sagged against his hold. He held her upright with great force, hurting her arms. Her father? Dead? "What of the isle?" she asked desperately.

"The king has taken it back and installed a new steward. Yer home is lost to ye now, Catriona. Either ye marry me or wait for the king to find ye a husband."

"Bute is safe?" Her deception was over. Bute was safe from the Norse and now under the protection of the king. Weariness seeped into her bones.

"Safe enough," he grumbled.

"Aye, now ye cannae get yer hands on it."

"But I can have yer dowry and ye."

"Nay," she shouted, her voice echoed around the hall and startled even her. "Ye cannae have me. I willnae let ye."

"Who's to stop me?" he hissed. "Yer on my lands, in my keep. Ye have no one to protect ye. I shall wed ye and bed ye and then ye shall be mine, pretty one." He wrapped his strong hands around her head and forced his lips upon hers.

She squeaked and scrabbled against his chest. Blood tainted her mouth as his teeth dug into her lip.

"What in the devil—"

Gillean broke away, panting, hands still compressing either side of her head to glare at Lorna as she scurried down the stairs. Catriona considered breaking away but the pressure on her head had her fearing he might crush her skull and be done with her. Her limbs shook while she tried to absorb everything. Her father was dead. Her home lost to her. The truth was out.

"Gillean, what are ye doing?" Lorna demanded. "Release her."

"Sister," he warned, "dinnae get involved."

"I'll no' have ye handling a lass like that under my roof." Lorna propped her hands on her hips.

He skipped his gaze between Catriona and Lorna. Catriona winced when his face filled with rage once more. "This is my castle. I have been kind enough letting ye stay after my brother's death." He finally released Catriona and flung her to one side, sending her sprawling. Reeds dug into her palms. "Dinnae tell me what to do in my own home." Gillean stalked toward Lorna but Lorna raised her chin, her stance firm.

"I have looked after yer home well, *brother*, and the men are loyal to me. Dinnae think ye can behave so and get away with it."

Gillean licked his lips and snatched Lorna's chin, lifting it. Catriona scrabbled to her feet and waited. Her heart threatened to burst from her chest and the tightness increased. A swoon might overcome her soon, she feared, as Gillean's behaviour began to blur with the Norseman's. But she kept her gaze focused on Lorna and fought to draw in deep breaths.

"We shall see how loyal yer men are when I have their mistress locked away."

"Nay!" Catriona flew at him, landing on his back.

With a grunt, he fought her hold on his neck. She dug her nails in but she was no match for him. He flung her off in an instant and her head connected with the stone wall. Pain blasted through her skull and her breaths shortened. There, on the floor, panting and wheezing, she finally succumbed to the darkness as Gillean descended on Lorna.

***

Finn scowled and Dìleas whinnied as he put her in the stables. He sniffed the air and shook his head. Something had put the horse on edge and he felt the same. He set aside the saddle and searched for a stable boy.

No one.

He stepped out of the stables and peered around. Men patrolled the walls but all was quiet—unusually quiet. Where was the cheerful banter? The laughter of men and the noise of a castle at work? He made to walk up the inner steps to speak with one of the men-at-arms, but Logan approached, his dark hair in disarray as if he'd been running his hands through it.

"Finn, thank God."

"Logan, what is this? Is something amiss?"

Logan went to put his hand to his sword and shook his head as his hand found nothing but his belt. Finn's frown deepened.

"'Tis Gillean. He has yer sister held prisoner."

"Hell's teeth, in truth? Why?"

"A disagreement. Over Katelyn—nay, Catriona."

Finn stared at the man. Was he addled? What did he

mean?

A hand in his hair, Logan sighed and drew Finn toward the stables. "Much has gone amiss this morn. Lady Katelyn is in fact not Lady Katelyn but her twin, Catriona. It seems her father wanted to use her to appease Gillean who was threatening war."

Finn sucked in a sharp breath. Katelyn was not Katelyn? What in the devil...?

"Gillean knew as much but intended to marry Catriona regardless. He hungers for her dowry, which is like to be plentiful, and, as I'm sure ye noticed, he hungers for K—I mean Catriona too. It seems Catriona denied him and Lorna interfered."

Katelyn—nay, Catriona—really did not want Gillean then. No wonder she had been upset the previous night. His mind whirled. But why had she not told him? Did she not trust him? "Why has he locked Lorna up?"

"He plans to marry Catriona regardless of whether she consents or not. Ye know Lorna wouldnae allow such a thing."

"Hell..." The blood drained from his face, a chill swept through him. Yet *Catriona* had deceived him. Had she not brought this upon herself? He blew out a breath and set his hands on his hips. He had been a friend to her, so why had she not told him? But then he had not been the most reliable of men either. He'd never declared anything more than friendship for her. And now she was in danger of being forced into a likely terrible marriage.

He snorted. Regardless of her name, he knew Catriona. The lass had a kind heart and whatever decisions she'd come to they were likely driven by good intentions. She loved Bute, that much she'd made clear. If she thought the isle depended on her, she would risk little, especially telling all to a man who was known to get into his cups or run at the first sign of intimacy.

"Have ye tried to get to Lorna?" He gripped the man's arms. "Logan, I trusted ye to take care of my sister."

Logan shook his head and tore away from him. "I can only look after her so much when she denies me. Ye are her blood, Finn. I have been here to tend to her tears and wounds, so dinnae lecture me of my duty. Gillean has set his own men at the doors of the hall. No one will go up against him while he threatens Lorna's life. He has disarmed us and we are impotent." Logan lifted his arms to demonstrate his lack of a weapon. "Gillean *is* our laird. None will help us for in the eyes of the law he has done naught wrong."

Finn scrubbed a hand across his chin. What to do? Since Alice's death he'd avoided caring for any women and now the two women he cared for most were in trouble. He had no choice. "We need to get to them, Logan. We cannae let Catriona be forced into a marriage and I willnae abandon Lorna to his whim."

"I agree. But ye'll struggle getting word to our men. They are scattered amongst Gillean's and I cannae say who will stay loyal to Lorna."

"Then 'tis just us."

"Aye." Logan nodded.

"I have my sword," Finn offered.

Logan laughed. "Well, then we shall have little troubles."

Finn laughed too and slapped the man on the shoulder. A lump still caught in his throat. What would Catriona be enduring in there? And his sister? Ach, if he'd only been around instead of behaving like a coward, none of this would have happened.

"Come then, let us see what we are up against."

***

Tèile fluttered anxiously between the hall and the bailey. Everything had gone wrong. Finn and Catriona had come together properly at the right time, so why had fate not played out as it should? And Laird Gillean was planning to marry and take Catriona against her will.

If only she had greater control over humans. It would make her job much easier. Alas, she could not kill a human, though she'd very much like to at this moment. She squeezed her hands together with a gleeful smile. Could she ensure

Gillean met with an accident?

Shaking her head, she let slip a sigh of relief and flew down toward Finn. Hadn't she already learned not to interfere more than necessary. If fate wanted Gillean dead, fate would deliver the blow. She cocked her head and listened to the men.

Why did he insist on being so stubborn? Finn clearly loved Catriona. If he'd confessed as much, Catriona would surely have told him all. The faery rubbed a weary hand across her face and nodded along as they discussed their plans.

Still, being a faery had some advantages. The men were up against terrible odds but she had magic on her side. Flying over to a small door—the one that hid the escape route—she eyed the two men stationed in front of it. They were armed—men loyal to Gillean. She needed a distraction.

***

Finn, trying to act natural while keeping his sword tucked in the folds of his plaid, led the way to the rear door. They paused before they reached it and feigned conversation for a moment as they took in their surroundings. Men patrolled the walls. While many were Gillean's, some were their own men. But Logan was right. Most were likely loyal to his sister, but would they go up against their own laird and risk death? They could not rely on them.

"There are two men at the door." Logan shook his head.

"We could take them out easily enough but without being seen? I think it unlikely."

"Aye, ye are right. Can ye cause a disturbance mayhap?"

"And risk being run through?" Logan shrugged. "Aye, that I can do though who knows what ye shall come up against inside the keep. There are but a few servants and certainly none of our men in there now."

"Aye, well, I've been up against worse." He considered the moment he'd infiltrated Bute castle and taken Catriona. Who knew his life was destined to change so drastically that day?

"I dinnae see we have any other—"

A shout made them both pause and turn. A hay cart, not far from the stables had caught alight and flames crackled their way across it with frightening speed. Men scrambled from the walls and hurried to the well in search of buckets. Finn scowled. There were no open fires nearby. No one would be fool enough to leave a cart near one anyhow—castles went up in flames too easily with their wooden interiors. Yet he would not complain.

Both men at the rear door abandoned their station and helped to tackle the fire. Assuring himself Dìleas was safe—the fire was far enough away from the stables and his horse was too canny to remain should the worst happen—he dashed across the bailey, not even checking if Logan followed.

Hauling open the door, he raced down the steps into the

dark interior of the passageway and paused to find his bearing. Logan bumped into his back and muttered an apology.

"It's darker than the depths of a loch here," the man grumbled.

"Aye. Well yer meant to be in charge of this damned keep so 'tis yer fault for not keeping the torches lit."

"Ach, there's no point. Kilcree hasnae seen war for a long time and we have no need for escape passages."

"Apart from this day," Finn pointed out.

Logan sighed. "Aye, apart from this day."

"Well, there is but one way out, so we cannae go far wrong. Just watch yer footing."

Hands to the walls, they shuffled along. The ground was wet in places and their boots slurped and slipped on the mud. Moisture and the scent of cold stone lingered in the air. With each step, Finn's anxiousness grew. Would Catriona be well? Had Gillean harmed her? The man surely had to be addled to go to such measures, but then he could almost understand it, for Catriona had surely addled him.

Finn cursed as his toe stubbed against a step. "We are nearly there."

"Let us pray, we are no' against too many men," Logan whispered.

"Ach, I am no' afeared and nor should ye be."

"Dinnae forget he has Lorna and K—Catriona. I will admit

to being afeared for them."

Finn clenched his hand around his sword. Logan was right. He might not be afraid for himself but for his sister and the woman he... he cared for? Aye, dread curled around his insides and twisted them until sickness pervaded every part of him.

They took the steps slowly and Finn found them to be slick under his boots. When he reached the top, he paused, eyeing the thin slit of light creeping around the wooden door. He put his ear to it and listened.

"Well?"

"Cease yer noise," Finn snapped. "I cannae hear a thing with ye in my ear."

Logan fell silent, save from a low grumble.

"I cannae tell. Do ye know where he is holding the women?"

"Nay."

"Ach, and I thought this to be practically yer keep."

"I do all the work, Gillean reaps the rewards."

"I know well enough ye dinnae do it for Gillean."

Logan smacked Finn's shoulder with a snort. "Are we to rescue these lasses or not?"

Drawing in a breath and curling his hand around his sword, Finn eased open the door and stepped out. The wooden stairs to the gallery hid the entranceway but Finn winced as reeds crackled underfoot. He peered around the banister and frowned.

"Where the devil is—"

"Finn mac Chaluim, I dinnae know why ye think ye need to sneak around my keep."

Logan released a soft, "Damnation," behind him as Gillean stepped into view.

"Finn!" Catriona cried.

Finn's insides curled up even tighter when he noted the frail figure clamped to Gillean's side. He had a hand wrapped around her throat. It took all Finn's willpower not to obey the anger surging through his body that begged him to power into the man and pound him until senseless.

"Ye'll drop the sword if ye dinnae mind, Finn."

Teeth gritted, Finn released the sword slowly, the clatter making Catriona flinch. He caught her gaze and willed her to stay calm. He did not need her losing her breath and swooning at this moment. At the same time, he hoped he conveyed his intent to rescue her.

Somehow.

"Take them to the donjon," Gillean ordered, motioning to the two men guarding the hall doors.

Logan let out a growl as one of them snatched his arm but Finn remained relaxed, the threatening hand on Catriona's throat dictating his moves while irons were clamped around his wrists. She wriggled against the hold and her face reddened when Gillean squeezed, forcing her to freeze.

"If ye harm her," Finn warned as he was led up to the stairs, "I shall kill ye, I swear it."

"Finn, ye are too predictable. Ye love nothing more than to play the hero but ye never see anything through. I'd wager ye'll have forgotten about this pretty lass by the time I've wedded and bedded her."

Finn broke the hold of the soldier holding him and lunged for Gillean but a squeak from Catriona and the tightening of the hand on her neck once more had him surrendering. He eyed Catriona as he was dragged up the stairs and along the gallery to the stone staircase. Only when they were hauled into the stairwell did he snap his head around and eye the spiral steps.

A chill swept through him but determination steeled in his gut. Gillean might have thought he had the upper hand but Logan and he were within the castle walls—a better situation than previously. He would not fail Catriona again.

The odour of dank reeds and rusted iron swirled through the atmosphere as the soldier holding Finn pushed open the door to the donjon. Lorna leapt to her feet and flung her arms around Finn's shoulders but the man at his side shoved her back. He debated swinging his bound hands at the man, but the drawn sword erased that notion.

Lorna flattened herself against the wall, the pale light

from the arrow loop of the tower room highlighting her filthy gown and swollen lip. Finn clenched his jaw until his teeth hurt.

Gillean would pay.

Logan stumbled in behind him and the door slammed shut, the clank of keys solidifying their imprisonment.

Lorna stepped forward, as if she might throw herself at Logan too but retreated suddenly, shoulders stiffening. "Logan, why are ye here? Why have the men not fought back? What is happening?"

"Gillean has hold of the keep now, Lorna. He intends to wed Catriona and willnae allow anyone to prevent it," Logan told her, no hint of his earlier desperation in his tone.

Lorna shook her head. "I barely comprehend what is happening. Gillean said we had been deceived and Katelyn is actually her twin sister."

"Aye." Logan pressed himself against the wall while Finn paced the small circular room. "A ruse to keep Gillean happy it seems. I heard his men say he intended to attack Bute and the marriage was to appease Gillean."

"Ach, I dinnae know why she went along with such a fool notion." Finn paused and eyed Lorna's lip. Fire whirled in his belly.

"Ye cannae say ye have never done aught foolish for yer family," Lorna reminded him with small smile, "but she should have confided in us. She must have known the truth would come out eventually."

Logan shook his head. "The king was to send men to Bute to help with its defence. Likely her father never thought the ruse would need to last long. But he is dead and none knew where Catriona had gone—save Gillean who heard word on his travels near the coast of her dead sister."

"So he wishes to marry the other sister now? I imagine her dowry is great," Lorna mused.

"He wants more than her dowry," Finn spat. "I never liked the way he looked at her. I should have acted sooner. He will take her against her will."

"Why have the men not risen up, Logan? Why did ye no' lead them into battle? Our men outnumber his, surely?" She folded her arms across her chest.

"Gillean threatened yer life, Lorna," Logan explained through compressed teeth. "None would rise up when yer life was at stake."

"And what of Catriona's? Ye should have killed him when ye had the chance."

Logan's nostrils flared. "Yer life may be of no import to ye but 'tis to others. Besides, while I may foolishly bow to yer every whim, *yer* men are still Gillean's too. Mayhap they dinnae wish to put their necks on the line for ye."

Lorna blinked and dropped back. Finn shook his head

slowly. If he knew Lorna's men they would have fought to the death for her, but Logan was right, none would risk her being harmed and none would fight as hard as Logan for her. He cursed inwardly. Why his sister seemed to be denying such a good man, was beyond him, yet hadn't he denied a good woman?

"Enough," Finn barked. "We need to escape and rescue Catriona." He eyed the solid door. "Somehow."

CHAPTER TEN

Catriona twisted against Gillean's hold and tore herself away. He let her, eyeing her with amusement as she stumbled. She rubbed her neck and glared at him. "What are ye planning to do with them, Gillean?"

A cat-like smile stretched across his face. "Whatever I wish. Lorna seems to have forgotten that this is my keep, my land, and I am the law here."

"And what shall ye do with me?" She staggered toward the stairs, hand to her head. The knock to her skull and falling into a swoon had left her aching and unsteady.

"I told ye, ye shall be my bride. Ye may no' be yer sister but ye have a sizeable dowry and ye are a fine woman indeed."

Catriona tried to swallow but her throat was dry. She squeezed her eyes shut briefly to clear the fog from her mind. Almost as soon as she had awoken, Gillean had dragged her to her feet and had a hand wrapped around her throat. Prior to that she had vague memories of Lorna being struck down and dragged away. She only prayed Lorna was well.

She glanced at the gallery and back at Gillean. His grin lengthened. "They'll no' help ye, Catriona. Why do ye no' behave yerself? Ye will have to act the docile wife soon enough. Once the priest is here, we shall be wed."

Hand curled around the banister, she retreated another step. She longed to argue back, but had no argument for him. Once he married and bedded her, she would be his and there would be little to be done about it.

However, she refused to be cowed.

She edged onto the first step, sliding her feet back. Her hand nearly slipped on the railing as her palms grew clammy. Her gaze locked with Gillean's and a tremor rumbled through her. He dove for her, swift as a hawk, and she screamed.

Turning, she snatched her gown and sprinted up the stairs, Gillean close on her heels. He snagged her skirts but she tore away and ran onto the gallery. Intent on the staircase, she did not hear him until he was upon her and she screamed again when he wrapped an arm around her waist. Hauled against his chest, breath knocked from her, a menacing chuckle washed over her. Catriona fought the groping hands as they tugged at her bodice. Her heart beat impossibly fast and when he spun her around and thrust her against the gallery railings, almost snapping her spine on them, his face merged with that of the Norseman in her mind.

And then she recalled warm blue eyes and hot skin. Remembered feeling loved and wanted. The Viking vanished, leaving the aged, red-faced, snarling Gillean.

"Get off me," she cried when he fumbled at her breast. "I had hoped for our wedding night," he declared, gripping her wrist and thrusting her hand away, "but I might as well ruin ye now. Then ye'll have little choice."

"Nay." She twisted out of his grip and shoved against his chest. It only gave her the tiniest moment of freedom but it was enough to wriggle out from her confined position.

Gillean grabbed her again and she swung for him, fist connecting with his cheek. He put a hand to it, eyes blazing. "Whore!" he spat.

Chest heaving, Catriona steadied herself at the top of the stairs. She needed to get past him and get to Finn and Lorna. She hunched her shoulders over, ready to barrel through but he lunged for her before she was ready. Dodging to one side, she shoved him and he stumbled, flailed and tumbled down the stairs.

Hand to her mouth, Catriona could only gape as he crashed down the staircase, limbs flapping and connecting heavily with the wood. When he finally came to a stop at the bottom, Catriona peered at him, waiting for him to rise up and come after her again.

Gillean remained motionless.

A shaking hand to her hammering chest, Catriona turned to be confronted by the two men who had taken Finn and Logan prisoner. Chin up, she affected her coolest look. "Yer master has had a heavy fall and could be injured." They stared at her and she motioned with her hand. "Well, are ye going to help him or not?"

Exchanging looks, they eyed her and one nodded. "Aye, milady."

They hurried past and Catriona wasted no time in running along the gallery and up the stairs. Cool air touched her skin and she realised Gillean had torn her bodice. Thankfully her chemise covered her well enough. She nearly slipped on her skirts as she navigated the narrow staircase and she fought for air once she reached the top. Slamming against the door, she fumbled with the lock and flung the door open.

Finn turned his head and scowled. "Catriona!" With a shake of his head, he dashed over and lifted his bound hands over her head so she was flat against his chest.

"Are ye well?" he asked. "Has he hurt ye?"

"Nay, I am well," she said against his chest, drawing in his warmth and strength. She lifted her head. "But we must make haste. I rendered him senseless, I think, but he may awaken and his men saw what happened."

Awe haunted Finn's expression before he released her. Lorna got to her feet and embraced her while Logan hung back.

"I am glad ye are well," Lorna said softly.

"Aye, I am sorry he hurt ye. I thank ye for trying to help."

Lorna waved a hand. "I couldnae stand by and watch him harm ye."

Logan peered out the door and motioned for them to follow. "We must hurry. If Gillean awakens there will be hell to pay."

Finn moved behind them. "Ye lead, Logan, I shall bring up the rear and protect the women."

Logan nodded and Catriona raised an eyebrow as she studied Finn's shackled hands. But then, she had seen Finn and Logan fight. Weapons or not, both were skilled warriors. Though her pulse drummed rapidly and her stomach churned, she did not doubt they would do their best to see them out of the keep unscathed.

They hastened down the stairs, Lorna behind Logan. Catriona nearly stumbled into her back when Logan stopped at the bottom and pressed a finger to his lips. Cautiously, they stepped out onto the gallery and Logan peered over the railings. He indicated for them to follow but no matter how carefully they trod, there was no disguising the creaking wood or footsteps.

The two men-at-arms were easing Gillean into the large chair in the corner of the Great Hall when they descended the stairs. Finn moved in front of them, forcing Lorna and Catriona back.

Gillean, a hand to his head, waved vaguely at them. "Get them," he commanded.

With a scrape of steel and cautious footsteps, the two men came for them and Lorna clutched Catriona's hand.

"Get to the passageway as soon as ye get the chance," Finn murmured as he lifted his hands in surrender.

"But…" Catriona protested.

"Go!" Finn growled.

Lorna glanced at her and tugged her hand. Catriona offered her a smile of understanding. Neither of them had any intention of abandoning the men. In a swift movement, they stepped around the men and inserted themselves in between them and the steel points. Catriona held her shoulders firm as she eyed their swords and the momentary flicker of confusion on the men's faces.

Gillean groaned from the corner. "Damnation, don't kill my bride! Just the others."

The delay was enough. Finn and Logan pressed through while their blades were down and kicked the men to the ground.

"Move!" Logan barked.

Finn snatched Catriona's hand and they ran for the passageway. The steps proved slippery and Catriona struggled to keep her footing as Finn forced her to move swiftly. Soon her slippers met damp ground, slowing her pace. The dark confines of the passageway made her eyes go wide and she concentrated on the faint outline of Finn's shoulders and Logan and Lorna's breaths and squelching footsteps behind her.

A pale glow sent shadows frolicking and she stifled a sound of alarm. "They're following us," she cried out.

Finn grunted and tugged her hand and urged her to move faster. Her skirts felt heavy, weighed down by mud probably and the cold confines of the passageway chilled her skin. Lorna stumbled into her several times and Logan cursed. The golden light of torches grew, bathing the dank walls and a bitter tang seeped into her mouth. Metal clanged against stone and Catriona pictured the men with their swords drawn and thrust out in front of then, ready to slice them down.

The slender strip of light ahead made her head swim with relief. It seemed to her Finn barely even slowed as they hurried up the stairs and burst through the door into daylight. Catriona blinked in the light and Finn dragged her to one side as they watched Lorna and Logan emerge. Logan slammed the door shut behind them and Finn released her hand to help him haul a water barrel in front of the door.

Glancing up at the walls, she noted a few of the men-at-arms turning to view them. A cry suddenly went up, though she couldn't distinguish what it was and one of the men flung himself at one of the others. Within moments, fighting had broken out—Gillean's men against Lorna's. Shouts and muffled curses rang out. Some men fought with their fists, others with whatever they could find. Catriona winced as a man was tossed from the walls. The brawling spilled into the courtyard and Finn urged Catriona and Lorna behind him. Logan waited and darted into the mess to snatch a sword from a fallen man. He grinned, clutching the weapon between his bound hands as he made his way back over to them.

"We must get the women out. Whatever happens, Gillean is still laird."

Finn nodded. "Aye, we can take them out of the rear entrance."

Hacking at anyone who came near, Logan carved a path through for them. Catriona fought the rising bile as blood stained the dirt and men fought for superiority. How would it all end? Lorna's men outnumbered Gillean's but they were still unarmed. She glanced at Lorna—who usually appeared so strong—to see her ashen-faced and wide-eyed.

They came up to the small door, hidden behind a cart and the men urged them toward it while they fended off anyone who approached. Lorna fumbled to open it, pausing to call to the men, "Are ye coming?"

Logan paused and glanced around. "I cannae leave the men."

"Nay, ye must come, Logan," Lorna insisted.

"Lorna, I have worked and lived with them for many years. I willnae abandon them. They fight for ye and I will do the same."

"But...."

"Go now. Ye wouldnae want me to behave dishonourably would ye." He offered her a soft smile.

Tears shimmered in Lorna's gaze and she nodded.

Catriona stared desperately at Finn. "Finn?" She knew what he would say before he said it.

"I shall stay too but we shall join ye shortly. Besides," he grinned, "I must get Dìleas. She'll never forgive me if I leave her."

"And I will never forgive ye if ye leave me!" Catriona declared as her throat tightened.

"I shall have to live with that I fear, wee lass. Now be gone with ye, both of ye. Dinnae stop until ye reach Glencolum. Lorna knows the way. We shall be along soon."

Lip tucked between her teeth, Catriona nodded. Lorna gave her brother a quick embrace but Catriona couldn't bring herself to. She feared she might never let him go if she did. Before anyone could speak, Logan took off and Finn followed, bestowing her with one more jaunty smile.

Lorna grabbed her hand. "Come, we must go or all this is for naught."

Nodding, Catriona gripped the woman's hand and they ducked out of the door and ran for the hills. They stumbled and climbed, helping one another navigate the rocky peaks around Kilcree. Weariness ate into her limbs but Lorna's strength filtered into her and she pushed on. If they did not survive, it was all for nothing. It would *not* be for nothing.

Though her feet ached and likely bled in her slippers, she continued on. When they reached the top of the hill, they paused to gaze down at the castle. It was impossible to see what was happening.

"Do ye think they are well?" she asked Lorna.

Lorna squeezed her hand. "They are strong men. I am sure they shall be along soon."

Catriona spied the doubt in Lorna's pale eyes but said nothing. Numbness seeped into her body, taking root in her chest. If she never saw Finn again, she wasn't sure what she would do. Even the idea of returning to Bute—an unlikely occurrence now her father was dead—did not fill her with joy. The luscious greens and purples of the hills appeared dull to her eyes and the sweet fragrance grew sickly. Without Finn, the world was dying around her.

In silence, they turned, still hand in hand and continued

their journey.

"I am sorry for deceiving ye," Catriona said when the castle was out of sight.

"Dinnae be."

"I am not sure I would be so forgiving."

"I know why ye lied. Women bear the burden of much in this world and ye have had to carry yer father's and Gillean's ambition. I dinnae blame ye."

"Does Finn?"

Lorna grinned. "Nay. Indeed, he is probably cursing himself for not seeing the truth and letting ye confide in him."

Catriona nodded vaguely. Did he really not loathe her for lying? She had caused so many problems for them and all they had done was show her kindness.

"Dinnae blame yerself, Catriona." Lorna pulled her to a stop and forced her to face her. The fair haired woman eyed her seriously. "This is Gillean's doing, not yers. If he had not done this to ye, he would have done it to yer sister or some other woman. But dinnae fear, he shall pay for this one day. For every drop of blood spilled, he shall pay." Lorna stiffened and Catriona held her breath.

Horse hooves.

They huddled together. Out in the open, there was nowhere to hide. Catriona cursed her lack of a weapon but even a sword would do them no good against a rider. A flash of golden hair and wide shoulders atop a brown horse came over the brow of the hill.

"Finn!" Warmth spread through her and she released Lorna.

Another horse trotted behind him, the reins held firmly in Finn's hands and Catriona put a hand to her mouth, glancing at Lorna. She put her arm back around Lorna and felt the strength leave her. Sorrow tore at her gut and she only imagined what Lorna was feeling.

Finn trotted up to them, his brow grooved with grief.

"Logan?" Lorna asked.

He shook his head. "Forgive me. He was cut down. I couldnae get to him."

A sob bubbled out of Lorna and Catriona flattened her head against her chest. Lorna did not cry but tremors wracked her body.

"We must go," Finn said quietly. "Many of yer men escaped, sister, but Gillean prevailed. We must get to the safety of Glencolum."

Lorna lifted her head and sniffed. "Aye."

"Shall ye ride with me?" he asked.

"Nay, I should like to ride alone if ye dinnae mind."

Finn offered Catriona a hand and helped her up behind him. She settled against his back and wrapped her arms around his waist. He squeezed her arm and relief mingled with regret.

"Come, let us go home."

Catriona wondered what he meant by that. Did he realise that, for her, home was wherever Finn was?

***

Moonlight lit the small chamber of Glencolum keep, seeping through the shutters and dancing over the heavy drapes and simple furnishings. Catriona shuddered beneath the bedding yet she was not cold. She swiped a frustrated hand through her hair and sat. Yet again, she was confined to the walls of a castle and her future drifted in front of her, governed by others. The tightening in her chest forced her out of bed and to the window.

Pressing open the shutters, she leaned out and drew in the clean night air, eyes fluttering closed. Her body ached—bruises marred it, but nothing compared to the agony in her chest. Her home was lost to her. Her family dead. As much as her father and sister had not been kind people, she had always longed for their love. Now she would never have it. She opened her eyes and surveyed the rugged scenery around Glencolum. The tips of the mountains glistened under the half moon and great rocks sat at awkward angles between them. More dramatic than the landscape of Kilcree, she felt an affinity with it. A need to run amongst the valleys and boulders and lose herself.

But circumstances trapped her. She'd yet to speak with Lorna but the lady of the keep, Alana, had assured her she had a home for as long as she needed. Surely it would not be long until the king found her a husband and married her off. All she had left now was a sizeable dowry—incentive enough for many suitors.

Catriona trembled. Enough to drive a man to madness. Gillean wouldn't be the only man to think he could command a woman with force.

And no other man could claim her heart. It throbbed as a reminder of her love for Finn.

She hadn't seen him since she'd been ushered into the chambers, exhausted and filthy, by a fussing Alana while the laird, Morgann, threatened all kinds of vengeance. Now bathed and in a clean chemise, restlessness consumed her.

A breath ensnared in her throat when her gaze settled on a shadowy figure. He turned from his spot on a low wall and faced her. Had she called his name? He froze and though unable to see his eyes, he surely saw her. Frissons like lightning bolts ran between them. She gripped the shutter edge. Should she go to him? She longed to fling her arms around those slumped shoulders and tell him of her love but she'd gone to him before. She could not keep throwing herself at his feet.

Finn rose, still facing her window then turned abruptly.

Catriona sagged, the thump in her ears her only company. The impending sense of loneliness crept over her but she held her shoulders stiff. She had seen off worse dangers and survived. With the help of a good man, she had almost overcome her demons and her encounter with Laird Gillean proved how
strong she could be.

A light tap at her door made her hold her breath. Her muscles stiffened, refusing to let her turn.

"Enter," she croaked out.

The squeak of hinges. Footsteps. Whispers of fabric and long strides.

Hands came upon her arms and spun her around. She released the breath and wilted. With savage speed, his mouth met hers, hard and claiming. Catriona gasped when his hands found her waist and pulled her tight against him.

Too soon, his mouth left hers and he stared down at her, expression grim, eyes solemn. She twined her fingers into his shirt and toyed with his pin, tracing the circular knot pattern.

"How is Lorna?" she asked when silence loomed.

"She grieves."

She nodded. She never understood what sat between Lorna and Logan but clearly it had been more than just friendship. Pain lodged in her throat. She had been so close to losing Finn too.

"He was a good friend to ye too."

"Aye, he was. He shall be greatly missed. He taught me much." Finn released a light laugh. "Ach, even in death the man is teaching me." Hands on her arms, he manoeuvred her over to the bed and bade her to sit.

While she pondered what he meant, he lit a candle and placed himself beside the bed. The straw mattress dipped under his weight and he grasped her hand. In the candlelight the true seriousness of his expression made her stomach churn.

"I have been but a fool. I have denied myself happiness and ye too. To hurt myself is forgivable, but to hurt ye, isnae."

"Finn...."

He pressed a finger to her lips and smiled when she couldn't resist kissing the finger.

"Ye have shown so much strength and I have been naught but a coward. Ye offered me love and friendship...."

"I lied to ye." she interjected.

"Well we willnae mention that bit." He chuckled. "Logan and Lorna missed out on happiness," he continued, "but Logan never gave up. He fought until the end for my sister's love and I will do the same. I love ye, my Catie."

"I am Catriona," she corrected.

"Nay, ye shall always be my Catie. A letter makes no difference. And dinnae distract me. Can ye no' see I am trying to tell ye something?"

Catriona giggled and reached up to trace her fingers over his serious brow. "Ye dinnae need to tell me anything."

"I do. I vow never to hide things from ye again. Ye are beautiful and kind and patient and, in truth, ye probably deserve better than me but I am a selfish man and I need ye, wee lass. I need ye very badly. I have been too scared to love anyone since Alice but, Lord help me, I love ye." His lips twisted. "And ye know a highlander willnae admit to being scared easily."

Catriona put a finger to his lips as he had done to her. "Shhh, my highland warrior. Ye need not confess as much for I know. I love ye too. I could find no better man."

Finn reached for her finger and used it to tug her into him. She ended up flattened upon him as he fell back against the bed. Catriona settled over him, warmth budding through her chest. He loved her. While she might have lost so much, she had gained more than she'd ever had before. Love.

"Ye will marry me then, lass?"

"Aye."

"Thank the Lord. I shall have ye taunting me in my dreams no longer."

She leaned over him, her hair skimming his face. "Nay, I shall taunt ye in life instead."

Finn grinned—that heart-shattering grin she'd come to expect from him—but true delight lit his eyes. "And I shall enjoy every moment."

Catriona rocked against him. "Shall we begin enjoying now?"

"Aye." He grasped her face and pulled her down to him. "Aye, I think we shall."

***

Tèile grinned at the sight and fluttered out of the window. The air felt clean, renewed. Fate was back in alignment. She paused and eyed the embracing couple. Yet something was still amiss. She could not have anticipated the battle at Kilcree or Logan's death but it must have been fate or she'd have known otherwise.

She flew around the square castle and paused to peer in the window. The fair haired woman sat on her bed, chin on her knees. Tèile had a decision to make, she suspected. She could return home, the glorious victor. Not one, but two matches successfully made. Or she could stay and find out why things had gone so wrong for Lorna.

A hand touched her arm and she glanced up.

"Come, Tèile," the purple faery said, "'tis time to return home. Ye have done well."

Tèile took a last look at Lorna and scowled before following the faery. Something was not right and she could not revel in her achievements. But a word with the *sidhe* council was needed first. For once, they would take her seriously.

Aye, she was now a great matchmaker. She smiled. All would talk of her accomplishments. And if anyone could bring Lorna a happy ending, it was she, the Green Faery.

EPILOGUE

Finn admired his wife as she pottered about the cottage, preparing their morning meal. Her simple forest green gown reminded him of when they'd first met. Noble blooded she might be but she fit in perfectly in his humble home. Odd how he'd not realised how empty his cottage was before.

"What are ye grinning at, Finn?" she asked as she placed a trencher on the small wooden table in front of him and poured a cup of ale. "I know well ye are hiding some thought behind that smile."

"Aye, but these are all good thoughts, Catie." He wrapped an arm about her waist and pulled her onto his lap.

Catriona giggled and swatted his arm when he tickled his lips over her neck. "Ye are due at the castle. Morgann shall wonder why ye are late."

"Ach, he willnae wonder. Many a morn has he been late. I am taken up with my beautiful wife, something he should well understand." She twisted and wrapped her arms around his neck, allowing him greater access to the column of her throat. "Ye know ye were dreaming last night. I heard ye," he murmured against her skin.

"Aye, I was."

Finn drew back and pressed a thumb to her chin so he could view her. Not a hint of fear sat behind those green eyes anymore. She eyed him boldly. "No nightmares?"

"Nay, none at all." Her lips curved upwards. "Only very pleasant dreams."

He caught the glint in her eyes and chuckled. "Indeed? And what sort of pleasant things do ye dream of?"

"Oh ye know." She traced a pattern over his chest and twisted her fingers into his shirt, holding him close. "My husband. In my bed. Between..." she leaned forward and tugged his lobe with her teeth making him hiss, "my thighs."

Finn groaned as heat rolled through him. "And ye complain of me being late to the keep? How am I meant to leave ye when ye say things like that?"

"Dinnae leave me then. I shallnae complain."

Standing, he took her with him, keeping her legs wrapped around his hips. He stumbled through the door to their bedroom while she pressed a hard kiss to his mouth. Laying her on the bed, he spread out her raven hair against the blue blanket and lifted to admire her. Finn flicked a finger over her nose and across the tilt of her lips. His heart leapt. To think he had nearly missed out on all of this. His life had been so cold and barren before. With Catriona in his arms he felt truly alive again. For this, it was worth the risk.

"Finn?" she whispered, toying with the braid in his hair.

"Aye, love?"

"I love ye."

"I know. I love ye too. To the stars and back."

She stared at his braid then flicked her gaze back to him. Uncertainty dashed across her face. "I dinnae want ye to worry for me."

"Why should I need to worry for ye?" He pressed away slightly and scowled. "Catriona, is something amiss?"

"Nay, not at all." Catriona put her hands around his neck and tugged him down. "But ye must promise not to fear, because, ye see..." She bit her lip and released it, making him want to pull it between his own teeth. "I am with child."

Finn blinked and shifted his gaze to hers. Had he misheard her? "What did ye say?"

"I am with child," she repeated.

He gulped and lifted away so he could eye her belly. "In truth?"

"Aye. In truth. My courses have not come. But, pray, come back here for ye willnae hurt me."

He shook his head and grinned while warmth spread through him. He took his wife in his arms and splayed a hand across her stomach. "I know, for ye are surely the strongest woman I have ever met."

Catriona had proved her strength time and again. He no longer feared the future. Whatever it held for them, these moments would always stay with him. Finn captured her mouth, treasuring the way she softened into him and vowed he would make many more moments like this.

The End

ABOUT THE AUTHOR

Samantha lives in a small village in Warwickshire with her husband, twin daughters and too many pets.. She writes full time, juggling motherly duties with Facebook. In her spare time, she likes to drag her tolerant family around castles.

www.samanthaholt.org.uk

Manufactured by Amazon.ca
Acheson, AB

14006621R00164